"Give me a firm place on which to stand, and
I will move the earth."
- Archimedes

Far From Home

Library and Archives Canada Cataloguing in Publication

Strowbridge, Nellie P., 1947-
Far from home : Dr. Grenfell's little orphan : a novel / Nellie P. Strowbridge.

ISBN 1-894463-61-7

1. Grenfell, Wilfred Thomason, Sir, 1865-1940--Fiction. I. Title.

PS8587.T7297F37 2004   C813'.54   C2004-905027-3

PRINTED IN CANADA

COVER ART: ADAM FREAKE

*BRAZEN BOOKS and PENNYWELL BOOKS
are imprints of Flanker Press Ltd.*

FLANKER PRESS
P.O. BOX 2522, STATION C
ST. JOHN'S, NL, CANADA A1C 6K1
TOLL FREE: 1-866-739-4420
WWW.FLANKERPRESS.COM

First Canadian edition printed September 2004

10 9 8 7 6 5 4 3 2

Canada Council   Conseil des Arts
for the Arts   du Canada

We acknowledge the financial support of: the Government of Canada through the Book Publishing Industry Development Program (BPIDP); the Canada Council for the Arts which last year invested $20.3 million in writing and publishing throughout Canada; the Government of Newfoundland and Labrador, Department of Tourism, Culture and Recreation.

Far From Home

Dr. Grenfell's Little Orphan

NELLIE P. STROWBRIDGE

a novel

PENNYWELL BOOKS
ST. JOHN'S, NL
2006

TABLE OF CONTENTS

Chapter 1 — FAR FROM HOME / 1

Chapter 2 — TEA HOUSE HILL AND A STRANGE BOX / 5

Chapter 3 — A FORBIDDEN VISIT / 17

Chapter 4 — A NEW ORPHAN IN THE CRACKER BOX / 24

Chapter 5 — TREFFIE / 33

Chapter 6 — A MORNING FRIGHT / 48

Chapter 7 — SCHOOL AND A FEARED ENCOUNTER / 55

Chapter 8 — WINTER / 61

Chapter 9 — WAITING FOR CHRISTMAS / 73

Chapter 10 — DISAPPOINTMENT AT CHRISTMAS / 77

Chapter 11 — MISSUS FRANCES'S BOXING DAY VISIT / 93

Chapter 12 — NEWS OF CLARISSA'S FAMILY / 97

Chapter 13 — A CLOSE CALL / 102

Chapter 14 — QUARANTINED AND A SWEET LESSON / 106

Chapter 15 — SURPRISE FROM THE SKY / 110

Chapter 16 — A SPRING VISIT / 114

Chapter 17 — SPRING AWAKENING / 117

Chapter 18 — THE SCHOOL INSPECTOR /123

Chapter 19 — THE GOVERNOR AND HIS LADY / 130

Chapter 20 — SUMMER / 134

Chapter 21 — SEESAW AND TRICKS / 141

Chapter 22 — NO PICNIC / 144

Chapter 23 — YOU HOP LIKE A GRASSHOPPER / 149

Chapter 24 — BARRED OUT / 159

Chapter 25 — A FALL IN SUMMER / 162

Chapter 26 — A SAVAGE ATTACK / 166

Chapter 27 — NEWS ABOUT GOING HOME / 172

Chapter 28 — PREPARING FOR HOME / 179

Chapter 29 — MYSTERY BOX ON TEA HOUSE HILL / 186

Chapter 30 — ON HER WAY / 197

Chapter 31 — A SISTER'S CONFESSION / 209

GLOSSARY OF TERMS / 219

*Inspired by and dedicated to
Clarissa Dicks: to the child she was
and to the woman she became.*

1

FAR FROM HOME

"I don't belong here; I'm not an orphan," Clarissa murmured as she fidgeted on the damp concrete steps of the Grenfell orphanage. She eyed the other children playing lallick in the grassy field outside the building. Shouts and laughter rose in the still air while she sat silently, her elbows in her lap, the backs of her hands under her chin. *I should be used to this by now,* she thought, *used to what the school ma'am called a heavy solitude that takes over a person's mind when she cannot do the things she dreams.*

Clarissa knew she had been sent to the Grenfell Hospital when she was little, and that Dr. Grenfell had operated on her paralyzed legs. She didn't know why she was sent from the hospital to the orphanage and kept there for almost as long as she could remember. She brushed aside unsettling thoughts and looked towards tall, skinny Cora playing lallick with abandonment. A magical thing it was that anyone could stand on two feet, lift them and run without toppling over. How heavy her own legs felt; how light everyone else's looked. Running was something Clarissa knew she would do someday. She clenched her warm, full lips tight with determination.

1

She picked up the wooden crutches beside her and, grasping the handgrips, leaned against them, her shoulders lifting as the wooden crosspieces slipped under her armpits. She stood up drenched in the glow of this sunny Saturday, one that had slipped away from summer and hidden in the dying leaves of fall, only to jump out like a surprise. She looked towards the bay, its waves rolling gently into St. Anthony Harbour.

A faint sigh of satisfaction rose in Clarissa's throat when Peter, tagged "bully-boy" by all the orphanage girls, tripped Cora. Her glare met his grin as she got up panting and rubbing her right knee. She plopped down on the fading grass of the orphanage lawn, and Clarissa called hopefully, "Are you ready to go up Tea House Hill?" They had not been up there all summer. The year before, the girls had sneaked up on the hill twice to play cobby house with seashells and chainies of broken dishes they had found along the beach.

Cora's mother, Mrs. Payne, the orphanage cook, was usually too busy to mind where Cora went. Rules were upheld by Missus Frances, the headmistress, but they were enforced with more vengeance by Miss Elizabeth. Once Clarissa was hooked by the younger mistress's stern, brown eyes, she felt as if she would slide right off her long, thin nose into the wretchedness of her punishment.

Cora had promised Clarissa that she would go up the hill today, but as soon as the girls came outside after lunch, she skipped off to play lallick. Clarissa sat idling time, tossing a big black marble into the air and catching it on the back of her hand. It was a game she soon wearied of.

"I'm tired now," Cora said as she stood up and scuffed her way up the steps. She sat down and opened her mouth wide, drawing in the crisp air for a good breath. She rubbed her tongue over a tooth that was turned and facing her cheek.

"*You're* tired," Clarissa said crossly. "I should be tired, having to hobble up and down stairs and hills on wooden legs. I wish I had your perfectly good legs."

"No – you – wouldn't," Cora panted. "Some days they're too tired; you wouldn't want my breath either. 'Tis days when it's heavy and hard to pull up from inside me. You know I've been this way ever since I had a bad cold."

"Let's forget about what ails us for now." Clarissa looked around, and then up at the high windows of the brick orphanage which had almost as many eyes as a spider. Her strong, healthy face broke into a wide grin. "There's no staff in sight, not even Ilish and Georgia. Let's go."

Cora shrugged. "We're eleven, old enough not to have to ask to go outside the gates. Playing games is no fun with bullies like Peter around." She scowled. "I'd like to trip him good. I will yet, even if Miss Elizabeth and Missus Frances do punish me."

Clarissa looked towards blond, curly-haired Peter, with his smooth, white face and large, bottle-green eyes. She decided he was nondescript. That was the word Miss Ellis, the school ma'am, used for anything ordinary looking. Now he was flopping his elbows at his sides, his hands pinching and pulling up pants that were always drooping like a rag moll's. *He's so scrawny,* she thought, *half a bullet could shoot him into the hereafter.* She wondered where he got the energy for his acrobatics: hanging upside down, doing cartwheels, scratching his poll with his toe like someone digging for head lice. She turned to Cora and giggled, "He likes you."

Cora shuddered as though snails had just crawled into her ears.

Clarissa laughed. "Come on. Let's go." She swung herself along on her crutches. Cora pulled open the black wrought-iron gates and grinned as they clanged shut behind the girls. They were on their way up to Tea House Hill, where Clarissa could look out over the sea and beyond its smoky rim, and imagine the place she had come from, the home to which she longed to return.

2
TEA HOUSE HILL AND A STRANGE BOX

The girls passed the few houses along the bottom road of Fox Farm Hill and the hospital Dr. Wilfred Grenfell had built. When they started up Fox Farm Hill, Cora asked anxiously, "Have you got company bread in yer pocket?"

"You know I don't believe in fairies," was Clarissa's quick retort. An uncertain look crossed her face and she added slowly, "Even if I did believe in them, I know that a bit of bread in a pocket won't keep them away if they want us."

"Never mind then," said Cora reaching into her pocket. "I've got some crumbs of hard tack. I'll throw them along our path."

Clarissa giggled. "Maybe we should be more scared of the Norsemen ghosts Peter boasts about. He may think his ancestors were Norsemen warriors, but all his father ever did was trap rabbits and foxes – and gun kittiwakes."

Cora shook her head. "That thing he wears around his neck on a piece of leather – a broken piece of flint, it 'tis. He brags that it came from his grandfather, and long-gone

5

Norsemen have the piece that matches it. He calls it a hag-stone – supposed to be lucky."

"He dreamed a story, or read it in that history book Miss Ellis told him he had to read," Clarissa said scornfully.

There was still a ways to go up the hill. Clarissa's arms ached as she balanced herself on her crutches to climb the rocky path up to and past Dr. Grenfell's castle to the Tea House. Her round cheeks bloomed into blushes like apples ripening whenever she was hurrying on her crutches, her green-flecked brown eyes twinkling under a forehead of dark curls.

Fallen leaves lay scattered like gold coins among stones in a path spotted on both sides with orange crackerberries on bows of red leaves. Here and there, the cragged noses of cliffs stuck up under the girls' feet. Brooks sang under crossing boards, their clear water alive in silvery movements. In this peaceful setting, the girls forgot the discordant noises of the orphanage.

Clarissa stopped to take a little weight on her right toe while she knocked the cap off a mushroom, the kind Missus Frances called a chanterelle. "Here's something for the fairies," she said, laughing. "The devil's bread."

Cora looked at her in dismay. "If you touch fairy caps and the fairies see you, they'll get angry and take yer."

Clarissa scoffed. "You can't go believing stories other people dream. You'll be frightened to death all your livelong life."

The girls reached the Grenfell castle standing in a dell surrounded by trees. Clarissa slid her crutches along the rutted walk and stopped to look in through the long windows of the large, green house with a roof almost as steep as a witch's hat. Today the windows looked like black sheets of ice.

Clarissa moved closer and peered into one window hoping to see Mrs. Grenfell at her desk and her little girl playing with a china doll on the floor. It wasn't a Children's Home, not like the one where she and Cora lived. Dr. and Mrs. Grenfell had two boys and a girl, though there was no sign of anyone now.

Some distant memory of her own family stirred in Clarissa each time she was by this place. The windows set in the tiny room under the peaked roof in the large house seemed familiar and she had a vague memory of sitting by a window in a house smaller than the orphanage. She wanted to be in a smaller place with people who didn't taunt her, a place where she didn't have to climb so many stairs. Sometimes she daydreamed about living in the castle with Dr. Grenfell and his lady. Mrs. Grenfell was big and strong and regal looking; on her visits to the orphanage she wore a dolly hat over a mass of fine, brown hair. Clarissa liked Mrs. Grenfell, even though she had an uppity air about her. She liked her because she was willing to give out a measure of kindness whenever she saw fit, and she didn't treat the children of the orphanage as if they were lowbrow creatures. Her face looked kind most of the time.

The girls went past the house, past Fox Farm Hill and up towards the Tea House. Cora led the way. Her blue dress and yellow wool sweater, against scarlet autumn leaves, was an image of colour and energy even if her breathing rattled sometimes.

The wind began to freshen and leaves rustled to the ground. Clarissa watched one leaf flitter at the edge of the others like a butterfly. A snipe's long t-werps echoed as the bird glided up the hill on a light breeze. The wind fell dead on the land and the snipe dropped to its feet. It looked around as if startled. Then it flew back into the air.

As Cora clambered up the steep path ahead of her, Clarissa felt as if she were a little rabbit trying to escape the snare of the straight leg brace on her right leg and the short one on her left leg, her toes banging against the uneven and slippery earth. It would be difficult to climb the steep hill, but she wanted to do it before snow filled the path and kept her bound to the low land around the orphanage.

Clarissa sniffed the tangy forest air, happy to be away from the stale porridge smells of the dingy Home. She stopped climbing to admire a leaf with a dewdrop as bright as a diamond under sunlight. She dipped her finger into the bubble just as Cora called, "What's yer looking at?" Cora never bothered with dewdrops, so Clarissa didn't answer. She continued her climb, noticing that the undergrowth drooped like a crinoline gone limp under a faded summer dress. Except for purple asters scattered here and there, summer's flowers had shrivelled to raggedy muffins, their dull grey heads bending on scrawny necks.

Cora slowed down and leaned against a mountain holly. She coughed loud and long, stopping just as Clarissa caught up with her. "Look!" She pointed to a spruce tree; its sap had rolled down the bark and stopped to form a brittle mass. The girls looked at each other and shrieked, "Frankgum!"

Uncle Aubrey, the caretaker at the orphanage, had told the children that frankgum would help their teeth stay strong and keep consumption away. It helped Cora's coughing. In the spring, when the older boys went to cut trees for fuel, they picked off the sticky lumps of sap that had congealed on balsam fir and spruce trees full of sap. The sap turned into a rubbery chew between their teeth. But this time of the year the frankgum was old. It broke off under the girls' fingernails and turned cruddy in their mouths. They spat it out, but the taste of the forest lingered on their tongues.

Clarissa leaned against white, lacy scabs patching a bearded fir and picked off black, brown and green strands of maldow hanging like hair on the trunk.

"Our dolls won't be bald if we can get enough of this," Cora said, her blue eyes shining. She gathered a bunch and quickly pushed it into her pocket.

Clarissa shook her head. "I don't mind having a bald doll. I'm using my maldow as her diaper."

"Watch out your crutches don't go through the space between the steps," Cora cautioned Clarissa when they reached the veranda to the Tea House. Dr. Grenfell had built the cabin lookout for his nursing staff. During warm weather nurses used to stroll up from the hospital to sit on the landing. They could lean, a cup of tea in hand, on the gnarled railing that ran around the front of the Tea House. Now the place looked as if it had been ruined by bad weather or prowlers.

Before going into the Tea House, Clarissa leaned against a large boulder and gazed out into the harbour. Here she felt that she was on top of Newfoundland. In the St. Anthony schoolhouse, there was a map of the island: a long neck on a thick body with several short legs hanging loose. St. Anthony was at the head of the long neck. Clarissa imagined sliding down the neck to the body, and into her mother's lap. Wind tickled her senses as she looked down at the sea and across miles and miles of it sucking at the land between her and her real home. In the distance, long, furry mountains lay against the clear sky like a dark beast between her and the people to whom she belonged. She visualized a table full of children. She could almost hear their chorus of laughter, the sounds of spoons against porcelain plates. Here in St. Anthony she wasn't someone's child or sister. A faint memory of her mother often tickled her mind like a feather. She felt her mother tremble against her as she quickly dressed her for the journey away from home. When she tried to tighten her hold on the memory, it drifted away.

She stretched her hand and covered the whole place: a toy village with almost five hundred people. There was the church with a steeple, and the mission school, with an upstairs library, down the road from the orphanage. Farther up were the houses and stages of the better-off fishermen and Merchant Moore's premises. Next to these were the cabins of people who worked for the merchant.

From the top of Tea House Hill, Clarissa saw the orphanage as a tiny box, the houses and the merchant's premises tidy. She couldn't see – behind the decent houses – the rotting boards in the straggle of unpainted, black shacks where the poor lived off their own faces or in the merchant's ear. From the Tea House, the whole place sat like a pretty photograph, without the chatter of children and grownups, the howling of dogs and the buzz of logs being sawed.

"There's the *Prospero*," Clarissa called excitedly, looking past a flock of snowbirds heading out over the ocean. A large schooner was sailing around the point on its way in to anchor in the basin of St. Anthony Harbour. Flags were flying from its spars; smoke from its funnels drifted into the blue sky. The ship was bringing passengers and goods, and maybe another orphan before the harbour closed for the winter. Clarissa had often heard The St. Anthony Band, as the husky dogs were called, answer the ship's whistle with their wild, eerie howls.

Clarissa dropped her crutches on the ground and settled on a fallen log. The stillness of the forest air hung softly around her face. Just then a leaf rustled and a bird's song rang through the trees. A white-winged crossbill linnet hopped beneath a black spruce beside the veranda as if looking to gather seeds for its winter cache.

Clarissa lifted her head and was sniffing the faint fragrance of Indian tea shrubs when Cora called from the Tea House, "Look what I found!" Clarissa gathered her crutches, stuck their crosspieces under her armpits and grabbed the handgrips. She made her way up the steps and into the house.

Cora was down on her knees. Her straight, black hair, usually drawn from one side to the other and held with a barrette, hung over her. Beside her were broken boards and an opening in the floor. Cora looked up at Clarissa, her eyes popping.

Clarissa eyed her cautiously. "Why are you puffing and blowing like a pothead whale?"

Cora's voice filled with wonder. "I've found an old box!" She leaned down, her hands moving quickly to wipe twigs and dried leaves off the brass surface. She straightened to pick up a stick lying on the floor. Then she tapped on the brass-overlaid box.

Clarissa peeped down, puzzled. "It looks like it's been here a long time."

"We were never up here this late in the year; leaves and grass likely hid it. But I can't remember these boards being broken off. Anyway, look!" Cora leaned closer.

Clarissa followed her look. "The box's got scenes etched

in brass and raised so that even a blind person can feel the picture and tell a story. There's men, some standing and others
sitting around a table. One man is drinking from a jug."

Cora tipped her head to her shoulder and squinted. "On
the side there's a crowd of men inside a place with brick walls
and a fireplace with some jugs on a mantel above it. A crowd
of ruffians drinking their pint and gambling – sure, that's what
it looks like to me."

"Well," Clarissa said, "Peter did say his father told him
yarns about an ancestor coming down from L'Anse aux
Meadows on snowshoes after the rest of the Norsemen died
off. If the man was a trapper and had a trapping path from
here to over the hills, perhaps the box belonged to him or his
relations."

Cora was sceptical. "There's no Norsemen on it. Sure,
there'd be horns."

"They didn't all have horns; it was mostly the Viking warriors who had horns on their helmets," Clarissa said quickly,
remembering stories she had read. "Some of them wore caps
like everyone else."

Cora hesitated. "I don't know if I want to open the box.
My mind's splitting into wantin' to and not wantin' to open it."
She tightened her arms against her body and looked around.
She whispered, "Someone could be watchin' us. I want to let
it be."

Clarissa shrugged. "A weasel or red fox might have us in
its eyes. Most humans are a ways from here. We can cover the
box until next summer and think about it, or next Saturday we
could sneak away with a hammer and knock off the lock."

Cora recoiled, her blue eyes like two china platters. She
whispered, "What if 'tis a fairy box?"

"A fairy box!" Clarissa's face screwed up in disdain. "I

told you I don't believe in fairies. I barely believe in imagining them."

The girls looked out through the open doorway; the sky was like an old man's face overgrown with grey hair and a grey beard, one dull eye visible. The wind dallied in the air like a ghost. It grew stronger, moving its fingers through the fallen leaves.

Cora shuddered. "I'm all abiver. Let's go. It gets dark quick in the fall. We got to get down before Old Keziah finds us gone." Old Keziah was the nickname the children stuck on Miss Elizabeth after she washed out their mouths with a hunk of lye soap.

Cora ran outside and gathered an armful of fallen spruce branches. She hurried inside and dropped the branches as fast as she could over the box. Then she fitted the broken floorboards back in place as well as she could. Clarissa got up from her stoop reluctantly. She slipped her crutches into place, and the girls made their way down the Tea House steps.

"Let's not tell anyone about the box," Clarissa said as they started down the hill. "It's probably just an old box with nothing in it but rotting furs left by a trapper passing through."

"I won't tell," Cora promised, crossing her fingers.

Clarissa tried to cross her fingers and lost her balance. She winced as her body hit the ground. And then she went tumbling down the steep hill until a tree stump stopped her wild roll. Cora came running with her crutches. Clarissa, dazed and trembling, hauled herself up on them. She looked herself up and down and asked nervously, "I'm not dirty, am I; I haven't torn my clothes?"

"You and your crutches can stand. There's no harm done," Cora assured her, letting out a sigh of relief. She quickly brushed twigs from Clarissa's red sweater and grey gimp.

They reached the castle, and Clarissa turned to go towards it.

"'Tis best we didn't stop," Cora said cautiously.

"Come on!" Clarissa urged. "I didn't see anyone home on our way up the hill. We'll look through another window."

"I don't want to, but you can," Cora challenged her.

Clarissa leaned in to look through a small window, lifting her hand to wipe away the mist that came with her warm breath. She gasped! Mrs. Grenfell was sitting in a large chair beside a handsome cabinet chock full of books. Rosamond, her little girl, was kneeling on a white polar bear rug on the polished wooden floor. She held a toy chow chow, his black tongue hanging out in a pant. The mother and her little girl looked at each other and smiled.

Mrs. Grenfell's hands were likely as warm as wool when she tucked in her little girl at night after reading her stories, perhaps about her father, the famous doctor who had come from England to build a hospital and orphanage in this place so far from his home. She would likely have read the "Children's Page" in *Among The Deep Sea Fishers* magazine to Rosamond. Clarissa loved the story of how the orphans got their new fireproof brick home. Grenfell Leaguers and friends in the United States, England and Canada had given money to buy bricks to build it. Clarissa stared so long and leaned so heavily against the window that she slipped. Her head bumped against the pane.

"Hurry!" urged Cora. "If Old Keziah knows we're bothering Mrs. Grenfell, she'll keep us from our supper."

Just then Mrs. Grenfell's face lifted as if to catch an autumn glow filtering through her window. Clarissa looked into her face. The woman got up, and Clarissa turned from the window. She had peeked enough. They had better get back to the orphanage. She was lifting her crutches over the dark brown earth to go down the path when she heard the door open. She turned her head. Mrs. Grenfell was smiling at her from the doorway.

The woman crooked her finger, indicating that Clarissa and Cora should come inside. They wiped their feet on a braided mat and followed her down a hall, past a kitchen and into the room where Rosamond sat on the floor playing with her dog. Today was the first time Clarissa had seen her since she was a bare-gummed, bald-headed baby in her mother's arms. Then, she had reminded Clarissa of the bald, old men who sat on the harbour wharf waiting for Dr. Grenfell's hospital ship, the *Strathcona,* to sail into St. Anthony. Rosamond had grown into a beautiful child. Her face had a creamy china doll look; it was framed by a mass of long, dark, curly hair, not cropped to her neck like the hair of most of the orphanage girls.

"You must not breathe on her," cautioned Mrs. Grenfell after Cora let out a raspy cough. "I'll get both of you a little something from the kitchen, and see how the cook is doing with the cracknels she's frying for the doctor's fish and brewis." She sniffed the air and left.

The girls stood nervously staring across the room at the little girl. When Mrs. Grenfell hurried back into the room, she gave the girls a glass of water and a molasses bun each. She smiled. "The cook made the buns this morning. They will give you energy for your walk down the hill. You had better eat them quickly. The cold weather is settling in; soon it will be a jacket colder. Snow, too, I am sure of it." She looked through the window and frowned. "The sun dogs are flanking the sun. Bad weather is coming and the leaves have not all fallen."

The girls finished their buns and emptied their glasses, and Mrs. Grenfell nodded at them to leave. They laid their glasses on a small table and followed Mrs. Grenfell through the hall. She pushed open the big, dark door. Her goodbye smile followed the girls like sunshine.

3

A FORBIDDEN VISIT

The girls made their way down Tea House Hill to Fox Farm Hill. Clarissa moved carefully through the knotted brush of the uneven path. "Someday," she said, holding her head primly, "I am going to grow out of my paralysis and walk without crutches. I shall be a nurse and wear a black-striped white cap or a white veil. Later I shall get married and be a lady like Mrs. Grenfell and have beautiful children."

Clarissa was not going to marry a doctor. The plight of other people was always tugging on the minds of doctors, taking them away from their families. Sometimes they risked their lives. Dr. Grenfell went adrift on an ice pan in 1908 and almost died, even though he was called a man of whipcord sinew and wire nerves. He killed Spy, Watch and Moody, three of his beloved dogs, and used their hides to keep him warm and save his life. Everyone knew that story.

Cora sighed. "I don't know about gettin' married. If men come from the likes of orphanage boys, I'd just as soon keep my distance. I just want to grow up – to be past my mother's shoulder. Even when I'm on my tippytoes, grownups never hear me. Anyway, 'tis no good to write the future in the air."

"It's getting colder," Clarissa said, looking up. "I can see the sun dogs Mrs. Grenfell spoke about – dusty arcs of rainbow bringing bad weather."

Cora let out a squeal and tipped up her head. She poked out her tongue to catch a snowflake, her pale face flushing. The first snow of the year was tumbling down in a shower of tiny, silver stars.

The sun became a dusty face drawn behind grey whiskers of cloud, and the October wind that had begun to stir when the girls were on Tea House Hill now cut them like a whip. Clarissa's crutches wavered in its gusts as she trudged over the light snow. The exertion of climbing and descending the steep hill had left a jangled torment inside her limbs. She was glad to reach the base of the path.

By the side of the road at the bottom of the path was a shack. A quarter moon was painted on the door, as if the people inside liked the moon so much they wanted to see it day and night all year. On a piece of board nailed to the side of the shack was an admonition in black, clumsy-looking letters: "Don't spit!" Clarissa had seen the same sign posted on a lot of houses and shacks. Some older men had a fashion of chewing baccy and spitting it on the ground or into the wind. They didn't seem to pay any attention to the signs. Many of them couldn't read them.

"Let's lean against the shack for a minute," Clarissa said in a tired voice.

Cora nodded and followed her off the road. Clarissa pressed her back against the small building, careful not to bang her head on the iron frying pan hanging on a rusty nail.

"We've got to get to the orphanage," Cora urged. She tried to mimic the tone Miss Elizabeth would use if she found out they had stopped at the shack. "I forbid you to stop at any house in the harbour. You never know what germs you might bring back to infect us all."

They turned quickly as the door creaked open. A white-faced, anguished-looking woman in a dark dress under a worn and stained frilled-neck apron, spoke in a flat, thin voice: "I didn't hear the twiddle of the pin in me door latch. Come in, why don't yer." The girls followed her inside the small, single-room house. Clarissa's breath caught in her throat as she stepped inside and spied a pail of slops under a bench nailed against a wall. A small child sat beside the pail, sucking on a dried, ragged caplin. The fish's head, with its dull and beady eyes, hung out of the boy's mouth.

Clarissa smiled at the child and moved towards the tepid warmth of a square stove with little feet. It was cracked and had a long chain wrapped around it, keeping it together beneath a long funnel that pierced the low roof. She imagined the stove falling apart, and a tongue of fire leaping to grab at the line of clothes above her head, and then devouring the whole family.

Clarissa noticed a framed portrait of the late Queen Victoria, white-veiled, heavy-eyed and tight-lipped, hanging on the wall of the shack. She thought: *The queen wouldn't have been amused to know her likeness was hanging in a shack.* Inside the glass, the painting had swelled from the dampness seeping through the hole it covered. Up close, the distortion almost gave the queen a smile.

Clarissa looked at a man sitting on a stool with a wool sock on one foot and another wool sock on a stump of leg. His face, the colour of an old penny, was drenched with sweat and grime under a shabby Cape Ann. A TD clay pipe leaned out over his lip, dragging it down to his whiskered chin. The old man dropped the pipe into his hand, leaving his bloodless lips half open as he looked at Clarissa and Cora without greeting them.

The woman who had invited them inside straightened her dark, heavy clothes and wiped her forehead with a hand that looked scalded and dried; her fingers were scrawny as pickled caplin. "Youse be from der orphanage, I can tell by yer dress," she said. "The Doctor is highly learned, he is. You'm lucky to be in hese care."

"And glad to be," Clarissa answered, surprised at her words. She knew that the orphanage, with its bright electric lights and running cold and hot water, was the envy of poor people in the harbour. Missus Frances often reminded the children that the Grenfell Mission had been kind enough to give them a warm and clean refuge. They were better dressed and better nourished than many of the local people.

A little girl lay curled on a barrel chair under a pile of mouldy-looking rags. She called weakly, "Mammy." Then she started hiccuping hard enough to shake her thin body.

"Here, Child," the woman said, lifting a wooden ladle from a bucket to the little girl's lips. "Nine glutches of water down yer throat 'll take care of dem hiccups." The girl slurped nine times.

The woman turned and pulled a worn flannel barrow down over the child's head and tucked it around her tiny feet. The girl grabbed the edge of her mother's stained white apron and sucked on it – mucus dribbling from her nose like a raw egg. Esther, a girl who used to come to school, stood in a corner looking embarrassed. Clarissa could see she was puffed up in her middle. Esther wasn't smiling, and her thin fingers twirled a lock of dark, greasy hair. She knew what other children in the harbour knew: boys and girls raised in the orphanage would get an education. Esther was smart, even though she came to school for only half days; her soft brown eyes would light up like the polished glass of a lamp whenever she got her sums right. The other half of the day, Jack, her brother, came to school to learn figuring. He told the school ma'am: "I don't want to be cheated by the merchant whose youngsters always got the smell of new clothes on 'em. Otherwise, learning t'ings I don't need to know is a waste of good earnin' time."

A woman, wrapped in a torn blanket, lay on a sack mattress on a frame beside a wall. A hole in one of her knitted leggings showed a bit of scabby, white leg above a bandaged foot. She was so thin and old-looking that wrinkles seemed to have fallen out of her face into her neck. When she moved to sit up, the girls noticed spots on her face.

"She's going to die soon," Cora whispered.

"How do you know?" Clarissa whispered back.

"You can tell by looking at her face. It's started to spoil – gone mildewy."

"People's faces don't spoil."

Cora shrugged, and the woman who had let them in asked sharply, "Don't der mistresses at dat cracker box tell yers dat whisperin' is der same as crackin' lies?"

"But we're not telling lies!" Clarissa insisted.

"Then speak it out."

The girls looked at each other. Cora said quickly, "We gotta go."

"Yes," Clarissa added, "we had better be going. Thanks for letting us get warm." She moved across the hard clay floor. Cora quickly opened the door, letting in a blow of cold, fresh air.

The woman put her hand on Clarissa's shoulder. "Sure, you stepped over der back stock of a gun. You better step right back or 'twill be bad luck in yer days ahead."

"'Tis best not to leave der gun on der floor," the old man called as Clarissa lifted her crutches to step back over the gun and go around it.

"Dat it is, den," the woman said, nodding; she glared at the man. She reached down and picked up the gun.

Clarissa had heard that the woman was given to charming. She turned back and asked impulsively, "Can you charm someone's life so it can be as they want it to be?"

The woman's sharp eyes lifted, seeming to travel. Then she turned and looked at Clarissa. "Take a piece of bark from a tree and carve yer wish in it, then leave it under yer bed. But never expect anything to be exactly."

Clarissa nodded. "We may come back again."

"So do," the woman answered with a yellow-toothed smile. From the stool the man called after them: "*Meeami Abashish.*"

Cora called back, "Goodbye for a little while to you, too."

The snow had stopped but the sky was low and grey. Clarissa was happy to be moving away from a home so different from the large, tidy orphanage.

The girls turned towards the cold breath of the harbour. The *Prospero* had sailed as far away as Boston, and was now sitting out in St. Anthony harbour, alight from stem to stern. Along with mail, it had brought passengers. Some were still on the boat, looking over the rail watching barrels of flour, molasses and oil winched down to smaller boats.

Clarissa wished she would get her own letter from her real home in Humbermouth. Instead, letters asking about her were always addressed to the headmistress.

As she swung her legs up the orphanage steps, Clarissa almost fell on her face. She was now in as much of a rush as Cora to get inside the orphanage and up the stairs before Missus Frances asked them where they had been, and punished them for not staying on the grounds as they were supposed to do – except on church and school days. The mistress must never know the girls had been in a shack where the man likely had no wages and the children likely carried lice – and worse.

Cora rushed on ahead while Clarissa regained her footing. She had to get upstairs and wash before supper, or there might not be any food for her. Cora was on her way down the stairs to the dining room when Clarissa left the bath and toilet room, which Miss Elizabeth called a lobby.

Clarissa was relieved to get downstairs and hobble into the dining room before the last bell rang. Looking over at the table of boys, she hoped none of them would wander up Tea House Hill and discover the strange box before she and Cora had a chance to get back there.

4

A NEW ORPHAN IN THE CRACKER BOX

Cora and the other girls were sitting on benches lining each side of the long table when Clarissa took her place at the end, placing her crutches against a stool. She sat facing Imogene, one of the older girls. Everyone called her Emma Jane when they weren't calling her Miss Tattle-tale. Imogene was always trying to get in the mistresses' good graces by looking for someone to tattle on. Clarissa hoped Miss Tattle-tale wouldn't discover that she and Cora had been up on Tea House Hill.

Missus Frances, a stout, light-haired American, looked Clarissa's way with a deep frown on her white face; her cheeks were like dumplings against her nose, itself a pinch of white dough. Clarissa felt her heart rising in her throat, as if it would choke her. She expected the whip of Missus Frances's voice to chase her and Cora to bed without supper. The woman's grey eyes shifted away, and Clarissa's heart settled.

Missus Frances lifted her head high and opened her mouth wide to offer thanks for the meal. The children looked at her, ready to follow as her voice lifted to sing the grace.

"Praise God, from Whom all blessings flow;
Praise Him, all creatures here below;
Praise Him above, ye heavenly host; Praise
Father, Son, and Holy Ghost."

Once grace was finished, Clarissa dipped into her rabbit
pie, trying not to think of the rabbit all in one piece, like the
wild rabbits that hopped among the trees across from the
orphanage. She stuck her spoon into the large tub of black-
berry jam on the table and spread a heaping spoonful on her
slice of buttered bread. Biting into it, she looked longingly
towards the stainless steel water jug, swallowing dryly. *No water
until you have finished your meal.* That was the rule. Clarissa
chewed her food slowly, hoping it wouldn't get stuck in her
throat. By the time she got to the last bite, she was so thirsty
she gulped her glass of water and got a stomach cramp.

After supper, Clarissa hobbled towards the stairs with
Cora beside her. The girls turned at the sound of the orphanage door opening. They smiled as Dr. Grenfell came inside
with a little blond girl by the hand.

Clarissa was always glad to see the Englishman, someone
the orphanage helpers called "the man himself", sometimes
with as much reverence as if they were referring to "the Man
Above." He seemed almost as important as God. The mistresses scurried about putting everything in place whenever
they heard that Dr. Grenfell was on his way. Clarissa knew he
wasn't God. Although Dr. Grenfell had used his knife and his
medicine to make some people walk on two feet again, he had
left her in pain and on crutches. She looked towards the frail
little girl holding the arm of a wooden stick dolly dangling
beside her.

"This is your home now, Trophenia," Dr. Grenfell was

saying in a gentle voice, looking down into the child's upturned face.

The door to the mistresses' office opened and out came Miss Elizabeth and the long sweep of her navy dress as she hurried towards the doctor. She smoothed dark hair pulled back into a bun and parted at the crown, showing an even line of white skin. Then she lifted her chin, her jaw as streamlined as a ship's prow, and gave the doctor her best smile, the one she saved, like good clothes, for special occasions. The doctor glanced at her and nodded. "Another child to be in your care, and Frances's," he said in his crisp English voice. Then he smiled kindly at the children running to gather around him. He listened to news about their activities until Miss Elizabeth, with apologies to the doctor, shooed them off to the activity room, where they were allowed to spend an hour before bed.

Clarissa lingered in the distance and watched the new inmate, one small, cuffed hand holding tightly to Dr. Grenfell's large, gloved one. The doctor was wearing a sealskin parka, its hood trimmed with white fur; only a little of his kind, rugged face showed. Seams ran like white scars up his sealskin boots, their tops tied with twine. Clarissa wondered what he was carrying in the leather purse at his side. Likely a knife and thread, she reasoned, a knife to cut patients open and take out terrible things like the consumption bug, and some thread to tie the skin back up.

There's not a blemish on Trophenia's face, Clarissa thought in awe. She stared at the bright blue eyes in that pale face, the blond hair under a round, blue cap. It was the hair of an angel. Cora's mother had told Clarissa: "Your hair is rich brown, like fresh earth turned up in the spring." *The colour of wet dirt,* Clarissa had answered her silently.

Just wait, Clarissa thought. *Soon Old Keziah will jib off*

Trophenia's hair like a tomboy's. The mistress had done that to Clarissa's thick, heavy hair after she came from the Grenfell Hospital. "When children arrive at The Home," Miss Elizabeth had explained, "their heads often carry creatures bent on finding new feeding grounds."

Miss Elizabeth was speaking quietly to the doctor. He followed her into the office with the new orphan by the hand; his sealskin boots chafing against each other, made soft whispers.

As soon as Dr. Grenfell left the orphanage, the little orphan screamed, "Mammy! Mammy!" Her eyes darted back and forth as if looking for a familiar face in this strange place.

Voices wrapped in silk gloves reach towards us when the doctor is present, Clarissa thought. *Voices without gloves reach like sharp fingers grabbing ears when the door shuts behind him.*

Miss Elizabeth's brown eyes narrowed as she looked back at Trophenia. "Your mother has gone to Heaven."

"She wouldn't go away. She loves me," the little girl sobbed. "But if she's gone to Heaven, I wanna go too."

"It's too far and you can't go unless God calls you."

"Mammy never said she wus goin' to dat place," Trophenia cried.

"You little heathen – you know nothing about Heaven!" the mistress scolded as she pulled off the girl's dark, shabby coat and Juliet cap.

The new girl looked so thin Clarissa imagined her shoulder blades turning into wings and flying her away to Heaven. She wanted to call to her, tell her not to cry. But she knew if she opened her mouth, nothing would get past the stern look on Miss Elizabeth's face.

The mistress warned: "Stop your whingeing, Child, or I shall put you in the broom closet."

The little girl's eyes widened and she began to howl. The mistress grabbed her arm and pulled her towards the closet. She opened the door and pushed Trophenia into the dark. Clarissa stared as Miss Elizabeth closed the door and turned a key in the lock. Trophenia's screams grew louder, and then stopped, leaving a heavy silence and a sense that the little girl had disappeared. The mistress unlocked the door and opened it. Trophenia got up from the floor and rushed out, emitting quick, shuddering gasps. Finally she stood quiet, shivering.

Clarissa hobbled over to her. "I'm Clarissa. I can show you around if you want."

The little girl looked at her. "I'm Treffie," she murmured.

Miss Elizabeth came between them. "Trophenia," she said, "has to have food and a bath, and then it will be bedtime. Perhaps tomorrow."

The mistress nodded to Georgia, a young helper who was passing by, indicating she was to take care of Treffie. Then Miss Elizabeth strode towards the playroom. Clarissa watched as she stood in the doorway and called, "All up now to get your baths and brush your teeth." Her hand seemed to sweep the children from the playroom.

Clarissa knew what to expect for Treffie. She would get a toothbrush, a towel and a face cloth, and an ordinary comb. She would also get a fine-tooth comb to hang on the wall beside her bed so she could do a regular check for crawlers. The last time Clarissa had picked up a crawler, Missus Frances had blamed it on her mixing with outsiders on the school playground. Her hair was cut, and kerosene, mixed with larkspur, ether and cottonseed, was combed through what was left of it. The concoction was left on all night; it burned her scalp. In the morning, Housemother Simmons came huffing and puffing to wash her hair.

Later that day, Cora's mother, passing by the dormitory, had found Clarissa looking at herself in the bath and toilet room mirror and crying bitterly at the fierce sight of herself. "Now me child," Mrs. Payne had chided, "sure, 'tis only to get the mites out of your mazard before they hatch and eat you out of head and skin. You'm lucky. In me mother's day, to cure the grippe you had to swallow nine lice every third day for nine days."

Clarissa wanted to retort, *Then there must have been a good supply of lice in the place, and no one to run them out of it.* Instead, she went outside the orphanage, forgetting she would be made fun of when the boys saw her hair. Ilish had put it in clips, making curls tight to her head like lambs' wool. Peter started the taunting, and the other boys took up his chant, "Baaa baaa, brown sheep, have you any wool? Yes, Clair, yes, Clair, a whole head full!"

Clarissa's hair lost its tight curls in a few days. She was relieved when Missus Frances told her she would be allowed to grow it to her shoulders.

Clarissa pulled herself upstairs to the dormitory, thinking about Treffie and what would be done to her hair. When she got to her bed, she dropped her crutches against the wooden trunk. They leaned there like wooden soldiers. There was no padding on them and they hurt her armpits, but they did get her places her feet could not take her. She was glad for that – grateful for what Missus Frances called small mercies.

She stripped off her clothes and laid them across the foot of her bed. Then she went to get a wash before the other girls came for their baths. She was too tired to wait for Ilish to give her a Saturday night bath.

It was a relief to lie in bed, her legs no longer swinging between crutches, her arms at rest from having to help her body get around. It felt good even though the horsehair mattress was hard under her aching right hip. In bed she could listen to her thoughts, instead of hearing older people's voices grating her ears. *Adults*, she thought spitefully, *act as though time is in their hands to slide children in and out of, and fit them where they please.*

She could be thankful she wasn't an orphan like Treffie. She would go home someday, although she wouldn't want to go home to a shack like the one Esther lived in. Sometimes her thoughts brought discomforting images of older brothers and sisters waving as she went down the path to a boat. There came the vague memory of a little girl standing in a doorway with a tear-stained face. A face she knew must be her mother's was clouded. She wasn't sure if these images were real or if she had dreamed them.

If she were home, she would likely have a sister to cuddle against in the night when winds blowing in off the sea rattled the windows like the hands of angry ghosts. But she was here – and with girls who didn't like her most of the time. One night she had heard the two girls whose beds were next to hers whispering too low for her to hear anything but her name. Another night, she woke to hear Celetta, one of the older girls, saying to the younger girls, "You can't trust Clarissa not to get up in the night and kill yer with a knife. My father said Catholics are cruel. Sure, you would think they were holding the Devil's mass by the way they swear at everything, using the Holy Name. Then they tattle all their badness to a priest and he tells the Pope and the Pope tells God. By the time God gets it, yer don't know how big a sin 'tis grown."

"But Clarissa doesn't do that. She's a Methodist while she's here." That had been Cora, defending her.

Clarissa had stirred to let them know she was awake, and someone said, "Shush."

Their words echoed through her head during the day, and she imagined that the girls were looking at her strangely. She didn't even know who the Pope was, and she wasn't sure she wanted to. No one seemed to like him at the orphanage or at the church where God came every Sunday like the Holy Ghost; no one could see Him but He was there all the same. He helped people when no one else could or would. Her Catholic religion was something she knew nothing about, something she didn't learn about at the United Church of Christ. A long time ago, someone had gotten into her bag and broken her little statue of the Mother Mary. Ettie, an older orphan, had said, "I bet someone broke your statue because it's an idol and anyone having an idol is breaking the Ten Commandments."

She was drifting into sleep when Ilish knocked on the door and came in with a fresh flannel nightgown, ready to help with her bath.

Clarissa watched from under the curtains of her eyelashes as Ilish shrugged and laid the clean nightgown on her bed. She left without a word. *She must have known I was tired,* Clarissa thought, feeling grateful. She let her mind drift to the strange, brass-sheeted box. Maybe there was nothing more in it than china cups and saucers for the English nurses' teatime on the hill; likely, though, the box held a trapper's furs and winter supplies – and spiders and sowbugs.

Clarissa sighed with impatience at the thought she might have to wait until next summer to open the box. Missus Frances would be vexed if she discovered her and Cora wandering too far from the orphanage with the bite of a winter wind in the air, the smothering presence of a snowstorm waiting not far-off. It was best to leave the box. For sure, it had been there a long time. Maybe other people had seen it, but they hadn't had the nerve to break the lock. She would open the box at the risk of bringing a curse down on her head.

She shook away images of the box and thought of Treffie, sure she knew what the little girl was feeling. She had come to a strange place where there was no one who had the same last name, no one who knew anyone belonging to her. Clarissa shuddered with the loneliness Treffie must be feeling. She pulled the bedclothes tightly around her, pretending they were the arms of her mother.

5

TREFFIE

Clarissa awoke to the clang of the morning bell. She stirred to the feel of cool air on her face. Missus Frances believed in leaving the windows open a crack all year long to let out stale breath and invite in fresh air. Sometimes freezing air and snow sweeping across Clarissa's face made her wish she were bundled in a bear's fur.

Without the bear, she thought wryly. Georgia must have forgotten their dormitory this morning when she went around to close windows and turn on the radiator valves. Clarissa shivered as she got out of bed and pulled on her surgical corsets, clean petticoat, grey flannelette drawers, Sunday dress and stockings. She was glad for the trunk that had come with her to the orphanage. She sat on it to get into her braces before putting on her gaiters.

Clarissa was moving sleepily down the hall, the clattering of her crutches on the hardwood floor mingling with the scuff of other children's feet, when her eyes were drawn to the sky framed in the window at the end of the hall. She stopped to watch as the day rose from its dark sleep. A liquid ribbon of startling pink was softening into a pool of light above shadows

rising as purple hills. The rosy light glowed off the dark harbour waters. It spread over the new morning, stirring and
stretching itself on puffy, pink pillows lying in a bed of delicate
blue blankets. Cora, calling to her to hurry if she didn't want
to miss breakfast, drew her away from the window into the
silence that came after the rushing feet of children.

Clarissa tip-tapped her way down to the dining room and
sat down at her place, staring at the hated bowl of porridge.
She had been expecting cornmeal and molasses, forgetting that
her favourite breakfast had been served yesterday, and would
be served again tomorrow.

Treffie had been scrubbed and her hair chopped to her
ears. She was sitting at the side of the table by the younger girls.
Missus Frances stood by the door in her Sunday dress, looking firm as she instructed the new orphan.

"Trophenia Premer, everything we do here is for the
benefit of our children, to see that you all grow into healthy
and enlightened adults. We have thirty boys and girls.
Although there are separate dormitories, the older boys and
girls come together for meals. There is a separate dining
room for small children. Your place is always in here. Do you
understand, Trophenia?"

Treffie looked towards the mistress and nodded.

"Answer in a clear voice, Trophenia. Here you will learn
not to mumble your words and run them into each other."

"Yes ma'am," Treffie answered in a hoarse voice, swallowing hard. Her hands fell to the sides of her woollen gimp.
She gripped the pockets with her fists.

"We must depend on boats to bring much of our food, so
it has to be allotted. Navigation will soon close for many
months. You must eat all the food on your plate, chewing with
your mouth closed. You will eat in silence. The left arm is to

be kept under the table while you use the right hand to eat. Our staff will cut your food, if necessary."

Treffie looked down at her green enamel plate as if her eyes were following its white trim. She lifted her eyes without raising her head; the whites showed big and curved under blue irises. Her thin, light eyelashes flickered as she protested in a weak voice, "But Miss, I always use my left hand. That's the way it comes to me to do."

There was no hint of leniency in Missus Frances's voice: "Here you must follow the rules. Those who do not do so are punished." She paused, then continued. "Other children came from across the Labrador Straits before you, Trophenia. They were not used to seeing food left on a plate. Some of them would eat their own food and anyone else's, if they were not watched." The mistress's eyes lifted to include all the children. "No child shall take food from another child's hand or off someone else's plate. Is that clear?"

"Yes, Ma'am." The children's voices rose in unison.

Clarissa's lips moved but she made no sound. She was glad when the mistress excused herself from the room, leaving Ilish in charge. Ilish the Butter Dish, a couple of the boys had nicknamed the plump girl behind her back.

Clarissa frowned at the bowl of the coarse-looking porridge. If she didn't eat it now, the punky porridge covered in cold, sticky molasses would be staring her in the face at lunchtime. If she left it then, she would face it at supper. She spread her brown handkerchief across her knees and, when Ilish wasn't looking and the tattlers around her were digging into their porridge, she dumped hers into her handkerchief and pushed it into her pocket. When the children were dismissed, she left the dining room with the soggy porridge against her hip. She reached the dormitory as fast as she could, and flushed the porridge down the toilet. She had done this once before, after a bowl of porridge she wouldn't eat for breakfast was left for her lunch. Then, like today, the cold mess had fallen from her bowl into her handkerchief in a shiny, round lump, leaving the bowl looking as clean as if she had licked it. She washed her porridge-messed handkerchief in the scratchy tub by the toilet, and left it on the radiator to dry. She would have her regular lunch and supper now.

* * *

Church bells were ringing, calling people to worship, as Clarissa hurried down the stairs and out the door to where Cora was waiting for her. As they made their way along the road, Clarissa looked around to make sure no one was walking close to them. "I had a bad dream about the box last night," she said in a tremulous voice. "I'm glad we didn't open it."

"What did you dream?" Clarissa asked eagerly.

"I can't remember." Her hand lifted to her mouth in a fist and she coughed into it. "And it seems that if I do remember, I can't tell," she added with a frown. "I'm *never* supposed to tell."

"Don't, then," Clarissa said crossly. She couldn't see why anyone would say they had a dream if they could never tell what was in it.

She struggled over the steep hill, to the beautiful, clear pealing of the bells, stopping to rest on her crutches and pull her coat tight. Cora kept on going.

"'Tis a soft wind gettin' ready to shiver across the harbour this morning," observed Uncle Aubrey on his way past Clarissa. The caretaker always dressed for church in a vest over a collarless white shirt and narrow-cuffed pants under a long coat. His grey head was topped with a quiff hat, making him look almost as distinguished as Dr. Grenfell. He stopped to knock his clay pipe against his hand. Ashes floated into the air. Now it would be cool enough to lie in his coat pocket until the service was over.

Clarissa looked towards a spread of fishing boats asleep on the still water of the harbour, the likeness mirrored on the calm surface. The wind livened and brushed away the image. The water's lips sucked the keels of the little boats; they began to rock and nod under a sky alive with clouds scudding like a school of mackerel. It was almost time for the fishermen to haul up their boats for the winter.

Missus Frances spoke from behind Clarissa: "If I had to struggle like you with your braces and crutches I'd go mad, and I've not near the miles left in my life that you have to travel."

Clarissa stiffened. Her lips tightened in resolve. *I'm going to be well,* she vowed silently. *I'm going to grow out of this.* She didn't know why the mistress didn't know that. As she hobbled along on the crutches, she often told herself, sometimes aloud, "Each step is taking me closer to where I'm going and then I'll be there."

She finally reached the little white church. The caretaker kept the door open as she swung herself inside, smiling and nodding thank you to him. She slid down next to Cora in the pew, steadying her crutches against the seat in front of her.

There was no sign of Dr. Grenfell. He sometimes joined Reverend Penny and preached, although he didn't have a licence. After these services, some of the parishioners would trot off mumbling that he should stick to games of chess when he wasn't practising medicine.

Reverend Penny was soon sniffling through his sermon on

Proverbs. "Give me Agur's wish," he said piously. "Let me have neither poverty nor riches."

Clarissa wanted riches and the full use of her body. Some Sundays Reverend Penny read about Jesus helping a lame man walk and raising a twelve-year-old girl from the dead. If God could do all that, He shouldn't have any trouble making her well. Cora needed more breath too. Some days, hers seemed to be stifled inside her.

There was a stir in the seat behind the girls. They looked at each other. Peter and some of the other boys were doing it again: mooching from church on the pretense of going to the outhouse. Clarissa sat listening to the sermon, knowing that the boys were having more fun sneaking down to Bottom Brook behind the orphanage to go hoosing for pricklies. She imagined them slipping their hands under the tiny, freckled water striders skimming across the fresh water. Sometimes they threw out an empty bottle tied to a string. After a time, they pulled it in with pricklies swimming inside. Often, they hid the bottle behind a tree and came back to church before the service ended.

Reverend Penny hurried down the aisle after the service to shake hands with the parishioners before they left the church. He had a pleasant face, and he always touched Clarissa's shoulder without speaking. Today as she made her way along the road, he overtook her, commenting, "My, it must be awfully hard walking that way. You're our little pet." She looked around to make sure no one but Cora heard him. She didn't mind being called a pet as long as the other children didn't hear. It was kind of Reverend Penny to say that to her; suddenly he wasn't just a sniffling preacher. He was someone who understood.

Clarissa always felt hungry after the Sunday service. Now

she could hardly wait to get to the orphanage. She was always excited about the Sunday lunch of baked beans and spiced, black bread, and curious about the pudding dessert. She made a wish: *Let it be chocolate, and not tapioca or rice.*

She panted her way up the orphanage steps and stepped inside. Cora had gone on ahead and was already seated with the other children around the long table by the time Clarissa came from washing her hands. She moved as fast as she could to sit as graciously as she could in her seat at the head of the table.

After the children had finished their rice pudding and were dismissed by Ilish, Clarissa called, "Come on, Treffie, I'll take you to the study room and show you some pictures."

The younger girl looked at Clarissa with large, clouded eyes, but she followed her into the study room. Her eyes lost their uncertainty as Clarissa sat down and pulled an album off a side table. She opened it to a photograph of Dr. Grenfell and eighteen children sitting on the school steps.

Clarissa grinned. "There's me. I was only ten then. And there's Cora." She smiled at the sight of the girl in the striped dress leaning forward carelessly, her dark, straight hair parted at the left and pulled straight across her forehead. It framed a glad face and a wide smile, though the eyes were dark and shadowed. One arm was over Clarissa's shoulder as if to show the world that they were friends, friends forever, even if they couldn't skip down the road holding hands like some of the other girls.

Clarissa pointed to Alice, one of the girls in her dormitory. She was wearing a light gimp and dark blouse trimmed with a white, pansy collar; her hands were clasped as if they were holding each other for comfort. Her face had a worried, heavy look. It always looked like that, even when she was doing things like blowing out her birthday candles. Alice was paired off with Ettie, who looked sensible and serious. Ettie's hair was parted to the right and pulled tight across her forehead and pinned with a barrette. Then there was Imogene who was older than Clarissa. Imogene stayed with Ettie and Becky in the dormitory on the third floor.

Except for Cora, the girls seemed to be in rack with each other, leaving Clarissa out. *They think they can catch my lameness,* she thought. She often watched the other girls go hippity-hopping down the road, holding hands and swinging them.

"Youse all looks to be a big family," Treffie said wistfully.

"You're in that family now," said Clarissa. "I'm sure you'll have your photo taken soon."

"I've never had my picture snapped. I wish Mammy and Poppa could see me on paper." The girl's eyes filled with tears, her voice faltering over the words. "Poppa was hunting – he got lost in the woods. And Mammy – she had the consumption; it drove the air out of her lungs and wouldn't let it back in."

Clarissa smiled wistfully. "There are mountains and the ocean between my mother and me. She's not an angel, so she can't see me. Your mother can see you from Heaven, you know."

"You mean Heaven's got windows in the floor? Sure, dat's a strange place."

"Heaven is a glass house you can see through, no matter where you look," Cora said as she came into the room. "Golden streets run right through the house and you can walk on them and look down to earth. I dreamed all about it."

Treffie lifted her shoulders and let out a sigh. She seemed relieved that the older girls knew so much about the place where her mother had gone.

Clarissa leaned her arms on the table and said in an optimistic voice, "One good thing about having your mother dead is that she can come to where you are without having to go by boat or dogsled. She can move lighter than smoke, and she can get you out of trouble. Mr. Manuel, the old caretaker we had here before Uncle Aubrey, said to me, 'Clarissa, yer mudder could do a lot fer yer if she wus dead. Mine let me outta a cellar after me stepmudder locked me in it.' He said it just like that. Your mother would have let you out of the closet if Missus Frances hadn't. Anyway, time always moves a punishment to an end."

"Pay no mind to the mistresses," Cora said, lifting her nose disdainfully. "Most of the grownups here are from away. They come to look after poor white and dark natives, and to look down on us at the same time. No one stays long – sometimes we get a nice one."

"Have youse been here a while?" Treffie asked Clarissa.

"It seems like forever," Clarissa said slowly, her eyes moistening. "I came to the hospital first, then to the old orphanage. From there I was sent home for a little while. Then Dr. Grenfell had me brought back to the hospital. That's where I met Nurse Helen Smith."

Treffie looked at her curiously. "I've never been to a hospital and I've never seen a real nurse."

"You should be glad for that," Clarissa answered, "though a nurse, in her white gown with a cloud of white veil framing her face, can look like an angel. Nurse Smith wore white stockings and thick, white shoes. When I was operated on, she shaved my skin and washed me with green soap. Then Dr. Grenfell put ether on a cloth and told me to count to ten after him, and breathe deeply. I went out like a light, and he sliced my leg open and sewed it up without me feeling a thing. I woke

up in a big, white room, and the pain was terrible. My hip and
leg were wrapped in a cast. When it got dark, I fell asleep with
my hand out over the bed. I woke up screaming – something
was chewing on my finger. Nurse Smith rushed in with a
lantern. I held out my hand and she looked at it. 'Shush!
Shush!' she said. 'One of the rats inhabiting this place bit your
finger. I'll wash and sterilize it for you. Keep your hands under
the covers from now on.' I was terrified.

"The next time Dr. Grenfell came to operate, I thought it
was about the finger the rat bit. 'It is your hip, Clarissa,' he
explained, his eyes twinkling as if he was about to burst out
laughing. When I woke up, there was a new cast on my hip."

Treffie's eyes followed Clarissa's glance down to her high,
laced-up boys' gaiters with hooks and eyes, and a brace that
came up to her left knee. The other brace went from her right
ankle to her hip.

"See, the brace fits into metal clips and is held by cleats. I
pull a lever up and down to bend my leg." Clarissa laughed as
if she didn't care.

"Would yer let me see your legs?" Treffie asked.

Clarissa drew back. Treffie's legs were perfectly shaped
from knee to toe; Clarissa was sure that under her knitted
stockings, her skin was unblemished.

"No!" The word dropped from her lips like a hot potato.
She didn't know why anyone would want to see the marks
made by Dr. Grenfell's knife. He had cut into her limbs
because she had what he called infantile paralysis and other
people called polio. Her left ankle was not only marked, the
skin was puckered. Her feet looked like odd socks.

Clarissa took a deep breath, and said in a forlorn voice: "I
miss Nurse Smith. When I was at the hospital, she often put
my hair in ringlets and tied ribbons in it, and she let me piggy-

back down the stairs. Then she would run back up and get my crutches. Sometimes she took me to her office and read me *Peter Rabbit*. Other times when I was sitting in bed waiting for my cast to come off, she would hurry in wearing her coat and boots and call, 'Come on, Clarissa, we're going on a sleigh ride.' And we did!"

Clarissa looked at Treffie. "I couldn't be too big of a crybaby because Nurse Smith always said, 'Clarissa, you have a sunshine smile.' But one night I couldn't help crying myself to sleep. I got punished for something I did when I shouldn't have or for something I didn't do when I should have. I can't remember which it was. When I woke up, Nurse Smith and another nurse were by my bed, their faces looking out of white clouds. Nurse Smith whispered, 'The poor little thing! I hate to punish her. She'll be excited when she sees these little, brown shoes.'"

"Did yer like the shoes?" Treffie asked eagerly.

"I loved them, but they wouldn't fit over my crippled feet. I cried to keep them to look at, but the nurse was firm. She said they would fit some other little girl's feet. When Nurse Smith had to leave St. Anthony and go back to the United States because of chilblains, she hugged me and told me to write her a letter when I learned how. She sent me a beautiful blue handkerchief trimmed with white lace. When I'm in bed and I feel the tears coming, I pull my handkerchief from under my mattress and let the tears drop into it. Nurse Smith told me that God takes all our tears and puts them in a big, blue bottle. When the bottle gets full, He empties it into the ocean. That's why the ocean is always full of salt water. It holds the tears of everyone who was ever born. Nurse Smith was the most wonderful person – like a mother."

"But you've got a mudder somewhere. Can't she take yer home?" Treffie asked.

"She will," Clarissa answered firmly. "Someday she will."

No one said anything for a moment. Clarissa's eyes clouded. "I thought I was going home after I got better from the operations, but then I was sent over to the old wooden orphanage. We didn't have flush toilets there."

Cora grinned. "But we had an indoor outhouse fastened to the orphanage. Wintertime, the floor got covered in ice. You should have seen Clarissa sliding on her skittering stumps. She'd be dancing to stay standing."

"It was the fastest times I moved," Clarissa admitted, tossing her head back and laughing. She stopped suddenly, sadness crossing her face.

Treffie's face filled with excitement. "I've never seen toilets inside a house before, ones with handles to churn water around and make everything disappear. That's a wonderful t'ing. I never knowed that water could run hot unless a fire wus under it, and I never seen lights that didn't start with a chuffie match."

Clarissa shrugged. "The mistresses spare electricity. They still use lanterns, like in the old place. Miss Elizabeth called the old orphanage "a home of rags and patches." It was built with green wood, likely cut when the moon was waning. Uncle Aubrey said that wood shouldn't be cut under a losing moon. The timber used in buildings shrinks, leaving gaps for the north wind to whistle through. Sometimes frost burst the pipes and we had to huddle together to stay warm. We moved into this orphanage three or four Christmases ago. The harbour boys make fun of it; they call it a cracker box because of the flat roof."

"Sure, there was a fire in the old place," Cora said.

"Not much of one," Clarissa was quick to tell Treffie. "Uncle Aubrey was accused of smoking in the furnace room, though no one knows for sure what happened. Uncle Aubrey knew I was worried about not being able to run if I was caught in a fire, so he gave me a lucky rock. It has a hole worn through the middle. 'Think on it, and when there's trouble you'll have the perseverance to run through it like water runs a hole through a hard rock,' he said."

Clarissa shifted on her chair. "I was beaten in the old orphanage, sometimes with a rope." She looked around to make sure the mistresses were not within earshot. "Once, when Missus Leah was here, she made me come into her room. I knew what was coming when I saw the stick with splinters in it. She made me lie across a trunk. I cried before she hit me; in my mind I could already feel the splinters. She gave me one hard bang on my bare behind. I think Dr. Grenfell took her out of there so she wouldn't knock the daylights out of all of us. I haven't been beaten since then." She crossed her fingers.

"You got beaten like I wus at home," Treffie said in a timid voice.

"You were beaten at home?" Clarissa's words came out all crusty. She cleared her throat.

"I got the stick if I didn't mind me farder." The little girl's pale face looked pinched, her eyes bruised blue.

Cora looked at Treffie. She spoke low and sad. "My father never beat me. The spring ice took him when I was seven. Momma was standing at the coal stove with a black frying pan in her hand. There were pork cracknels in it, hot and popping; she was looking through the window for Pappa to come home with some fish to fry. That first night he was gone I imagined him floating under the ice into the mouth of a whale; the whale would swish him around a bit and then spew him like the whale spewed Jonah in the Bible story. Uncle

Sims and my cousin Jim found him the next day tangled in a
fish net with ose eggs and starfish. They brought him into our
house wrapped in brin. Then they made a box and laid him
down in it, with his face covered in a white shroud. Uncle Sims
let me touch his hand; it was as cold as a fish. People said they
were staying up all night to wake Pappa. I went to bed thinking
he would be awake in the morning. When daylight showed, I
ran out to touch his hand. It was still key-cold, and I let out a
scream that frightened meself. I never paid any attention to
people talking about waking the dead after that. 'Twas all a lie.
Pappa had sold the fish he had caught the summer before to
pay the merchant, thinking to get more fish in the spring.
We'd have starved if Dr. Grenfell hadn't come and taken us
to the orphanage."

"You can manage here," Clarissa told Treffie. "You can
run and play games like hide-and-seek." She noticed a string of
buttons on fish twine around the girl's arm. "You can play but-
ton-the-button and always have the button." She laughed.

"They might come in handy here if you lose a button off
yer clothes," Cora said.

Treffie stiffened. "I'm keeping 'em," she said firmly.
"Dey's me memory buttons. Before me family died, dey put a
memory in every button, and when I touch 'em, good memories come." She fingered a large one. "Dis big dodger
belonged to me farder's overcoat. He would hold me against
his coat, and I would feel warm even if it wus cold." Her finger moved to a small, delicate button. "Dis sparkly one come
from me little sister Sarah's dress; she died of the fever."
Treffie's eyes clouded with loss. "Dis pearl button wus from
me mudder's favourite dress. Me buttons reminds me I wasn't
always an orphan."

"I'm not a real orphan," Clarissa said with a lift of her

chin, "even if Dr. Grenfell made me one by bringing me here and leaving me. I have parents and sisters and brothers beyond the waters." She looked at Cora. "And you're only half an orphan. You got your mother, your sister Suzy and your brother Owen."

Cora nodded, and the girls sat together staring ahead as if they were thinking things too deep to lift in words from dark places inside them. No one spoke for a long time.

6

A MORNING FRIGHT

Clarissa surfaced from sleep with a jerk, not sure if it was the morning bell or the elephant that woke her. She had been rushing to close the dormitory window against a creature that was big enough to crush the orphanage. She smiled in relief. The elephant chasing the orphanage as it rolled down over a hill on cartwheels wasn't real.

The senseless dream flew out of her mind and a shudder slid down her curved spine. She had wet her bed, something she hadn't done in a long time. Narah and Alice, whose beds were next to hers, used to spy on her. They would wait until they thought she was asleep. Then they would reach their hands under her bedclothes. In the morning they would rush off and tattle to the mistress that she had peed. Clarissa could see the glint in their eyes when the mistress pulled her night-clothes back and whipped her wide awake with a doubled rope.

Now her long fingers came away from a warm, moist spot beneath her. She stared ahead, motionless, alarmed that any movement would waft a scent through the cold air, and the tattlers' senses would stir to it.

"You must try harder, Clarissa. Pull your muscles tight down below." That's what Miss Elizabeth said to her time after time, standing there with the rope slapper dangling on her arm. She had stared back at the mistress, feeling the after-burn of the rope on her bottom, angry that the woman had added red marks to the white scar Dr. Grenfell's knife had left on her hip.

She had strained to pull her in-between place up inside her like a stopper on a hot water bottle, wanting to pull tight enough to hurt it for betraying her. She had promised herself over and over that she would never wet the bed again, but when her mind went to sleep, it seemed that her body forgot the promise, and she would awake to the feel of wetness and a dread creeping through her whole body.

Now she waited for the morning bell to clang, and for the other girls to finish in the bath and toilet room. When they had gone down to breakfast and there was silence, she slid out of bed. She gasped at the sight of red stains on her night-clothes, and a red dribble down her lame leg. Her insides were leaking out from her in-between place. "I'm dying," she told her wide-eyed face in the mirror. "I will probably be gone before Cora and Treffie, and the children in the infirmary who have consumption." Her eyes stared back at her like dark pools she could drown in. "I'll probably go to the Protestant side of Heaven and my parents won't ever find me."

She hurried to wash herself with thick, brown toilet paper, thinking she would come back after breakfast and wash out the stains on the sheets – if she didn't die first. There was a mesmerizing stillness inside her head as she folded a brown handkerchief and put it in the crotch of her flannelette drawers.

She made her way as fast as she could downstairs before

the mistresses had a chance to send her back to her room for being late. The bully boys and the busy noshers would all be sorry when she died. They would write poems about her and think of her with a measure of charity. If she could do it, they would hear her crutches thumping through the hall at night as payment for all the mean things they had said and done to her. Her ghost would knock them over the head with the crutches and they would sit up in bed sniffling. Cora and Treffie were the only children she wouldn't scare.

When she passed the office after breakfast, Missus Frances was standing in the doorway looking in her direction. She crooked a finger, the signal for Clarissa to follow her inside. "If I'm going to die, let it be now," Clarissa prayed, looking up as she made her way to a chair. She sat down and faced Missus Frances across the desk.

"Clarissa," the mistress began, giving her a serious look, "Housemother Simmons reports that when she went to change the beds in your dormitory, your sheets were stained."

Clarissa looked back at the mistress. Then she let her eyelids drop to hide the guilt she felt. She had hugged her insides in and had stopped picking piss-a-beds after she'd heard they made children wet their beds, and now something even more horrible had happened to her. The red dwarf she had read about in a library book *The Norseman's Tale* must have put a curse on her. It was likely his box she and Cora had discovered on Tea House Hill.

"You might not understand this now," the mistress said, "but you have two places inside your body that hold eggs."

"Eggs!" Clarissa's eyes widened. Her chin shot up. "Like a hen!" She swallowed, wondering how many eggs were sitting inside her, and why none of them had broken before – considering all the times she had fallen down. She'd have to be careful from now on, so they wouldn't burst again and run out of her, yellow and snotty-white – or bloody.

"What happens to the shells?" Clarissa asked in an uncomfortable voice.

"We are speaking of humans now, not hens," Missus Frances said sternly. A pink flush moved up the mistress's face. "Every month from now on, the eggs will break and there will be blood for a few days. When you get married, the eggs left inside you will turn into babies." The mistress pushed back her chair and stood up, instructing Clarissa to stay put until she came back.

Clarissa waited on the large wooden chair, her arms tight against her body. "I will never be the same again," she murmured. "Something much worse than wetting the bed has happened, something worse than dying." But then she began to think about it. If this had happened to her, it must have happened to the prim and proper Missus Frances. And it would happen to the other girls in her room. What a surprise they were going to get; she could hardly wait. She felt a laugh bubble up. Her lips were ready to burst apart in a wide smile when she saw Missus Frances coming back. She was holding out white flannelette napkins. "You are to pin these inside your bloomers, and change them as often as is necessary. Make sure you wash yourself down there after every change," she said in a tight voice. "You will find clean undergarments on your bed." She placed some silver pins in the pocket of Clarissa's gimp. "Now you will move up to the next floor to be with the other girls who are growing into women."

"Oh no!" Clarissa cried in dismay. "Another set of stairs to climb."

"Exercise," said Missus Frances, "is always good for the limbs. Ilish will bring you your belongings later."

Clarissa knew Cora would be a true friend and bring up her treasure bag of secret things which was hidden under the mattress in her old room. She especially wanted her blue handkerchief and the piece of bark with her wish to go home written in it.

"If you have stomach cramps, rest until lunchtime," the mistress called after her. "After all, it's Saturday. The other girls can do your dusting."

Clarissa now had another iron railing to totter against, or lean on for a rest before she got to her room. She thought about Missus Frances's strange words as she struggled up the layers of steps, up past her floor – away from Cora. She felt as tipsy as a lamb must feel after feeding on gowithy bushes. She hadn't known there were eggs inside her, and the mistress didn't explain about the shells. Were the broken ones scraping her insides – causing the tearing feeling in her belly?

By the time Clarissa got to the dormitory, Ilish had finished making her bed by the window. The young helper gave Clarissa a sympathetic smile as she left the room.

Clarissa fell across the bed and lay there holding her crutches and the napkins. She wondered what would happen to her other eggs if she never got married. Would they keep breaking and dropping out of her until they were all gone? Esther, who lived in the shack down the road, was pooked out and set to have a baby all on her own without marrying anyone.

Clarissa stayed in the dormitory until the supper bell rang. When she went down to supper, no one acted as if they knew something strange had happened to her. She breathed a sigh of relief. All kinds of questions about her body piled on top of each other until she felt as if her head would burst and scatter them. She imagined black letters floating in the air, and Peter grabbing them and putting them together in words she could never speak aloud. She was relieved when supper was over and she could start back upstairs. She wanted to tell Cora that Missus Frances had moved her upstairs with Imogene, but Cora had stopped to talk with Ettie. Besides, she wouldn't be able to give her the reason. Not yet. They never discussed the things about their bodies that made them girls.

Clarissa got ready for bed, pulling a fresh nightdress over her head. She was smoothing it down around her when she felt a bump. Her nipple was like a raspberry bud above skin that looked swollen – as if a bee had stung her. The other side hadn't changed.

That night the older girls came into the room whispering. They were not even polite to her; they talked among themselves as if she weren't there. They were still whispering as they got ready for bed and snuggled under the sheets. *Maybe they believe my brain is not as clever as theirs,* she thought. *But I'm quick enough to notice they're growing bumps like mine, only a little bigger – and on both sides.*

The next morning Clarissa woke up to dust dancing in sunbeams that fell in a slant over her head from the high window. She felt better, almost happy, until a black spot on the white wall started to move. She let out a scream, her eyes fixed on a black spider.

Celetta, the girl who had moved from Clarissa's dormitory the year before, was in the bed next to hers. Her head shot up off her pillow and she glared at Clarissa. "Fraidy-cat."

Imogene, in the next bed, simpered, "Oh it's so b-i-i-g. Knock it over the head with your crutch, why don't you?" Becky, a quiet girl with thin, black hair and freckles the boys called cow dabs, looked at Clarissa without saying a word.

"Devilskins," Clarissa called back, sure that they didn't

want her in the room with them because she was a cripple. She would show them. Her body was curving more and more like theirs, and she was growing breasts like them, even if it was one at a time. She drew in a deep breath and thought: *Maybe this is the year I will grow out of being crippled.*

7

SCHOOL AND A FEARED ENCOUNTER

Clarissa's clean change of blouse and gimp lay on the foot of her bed as it did every Monday morning. She leaned against the basin in the bath and toilet room, brushing her teeth and washing her face and hands, careful to clean the sleep crusting the corner of her eyes for fear the mistresses would notice. Then she sat on her trunk and stripped off her nightdress, glad that Georgia had been around to close the window and turn on the radiator heat. Still, she shuddered as she pulled on her clothes. The other girls had dressed and pushed their feet into their boots almost in a blink. It took Clarissa a long time to clip her braces and buckle her gaiters. She wished she could wear Beanie boots like the other children, who were nicknamed Beanies by the harbour children.

"Prune feet," the orphans retorted, remembering how wet and prune-like their feet became in mild weather, before rubber bottoms were attached to their sealskin leggings.

Once breakfast was over, the children hurried to their wooden lockers. They lifted the covers and pulled out their outdoor clothes. Now that the weather had turned cold, the

children wore waist-length canvas dickeys over their regular
jackets. Clarissa felt warm and cosy inside her hooded dickey,
trimmed with a white and red binding. She hauled on her
double woollen mitts and then her sealskin overcuffs. The
snow that had fallen while she and Cora were coming from
Tea House Hill had disappeared like ice cream on a warm
tongue. Still, it was cold outside.

Clarissa walked to school alone, except during the winter
months when she was dragged on a sled. The other children,
including Cora, went running to play lallick before the school
bell rang. It took Clarissa a while to hobble down the steps of
the orphanage, out through the gates, and past the hospital.
Then she had a steep hill to go down. At the top of the hill was
St. Anthony Inn, where summer volunteers from away stayed
while they worked for Dr. Grenfell on odd jobs around the
hospital. Clarissa dragged her body past The United Church
of Christ, and then beyond the graveyard. She turned in to the
two-room schoolhouse: one room for the little children and
one for the older ones. It was the last building on the point,
high above the sea. Most of the children could read the large,
white scripture sign on the Grenfell Mission School: "And all
thy children shall be taught of the Lord: and great shall be the
peace of thy children." Isaiah 54:13.

There were six steps for Clarissa's crutches to swing her over
before she got inside the school. Miss Ellis, a tall woman who
looked as limbed-out as an old tree with only a couple of shaky
branches left on it, was out on the step shaking a wooden-handled
brass bell as if she were ringing away a minute with each shake.
Clarissa tried to hurry for fear she would have to go stand in the
corner if the bell stopped before she reached the steps. She was
relieved that they weren't slippery enough to make her late. The
school ma'am's hand fell to her side just as Clarissa got to the door.

Inside the school, Billy, a harbour boy, was waddling ahead of Clarissa, legs bent, knees touching. His greasy black hair fell down both sides of his face like tattered fringes on a blanket. Clarissa cringed as the boy went past the school ma'am's desk, hard knobs dropping out the legs of his pants and hitting the wooden floor. The pupils pretended not to notice except for Jakot, nicknamed Jake, The Great Big Snake, who sniggered. Miss Ellis ordered him to shovel up Billy's mess and throw it into the stove. Jakot lifted the shovel from the coal scuttle with a look of disgust at the boy he called a knee-knocked, stinking buck. Clarissa felt sorry for the boy who couldn't help dropping his poo or letting pee pool under his feet in front of people. But she didn't want to be his friend – didn't ever want to sit on the seat he sat on any more than anyone else did. Even Miss Ellis looked at Billy as if he was the only one who ever made a stink or dropped a string of mucus from his nose.

Clarissa sat with other girls, some her age and some younger, at a long wooden desk. There had been so much for her to learn since she started school when she was nine – so much catching up. It didn't take her long to learn that the black markings of the alphabet could be named and strung into words, and words shaped into stories. She had discovered that there was no end to what she could do with words when her imagination got hold of them.

If she hadn't read it with her own eyes, Clarissa would have scoffed at the story of the earth moving around the sun. It didn't seem possible that the earth, so big, so still and solid under her crutches, could move so gently under her that she didn't even notice, and that it was because of this movement that the sun and the moon seemed to pop up in the sky, disappear, and rebound. She liked to lie on the grass in the summer and in the snow in winter watching clouds. Sometimes they moved across the sky like sails on ghostly ships, and then the sails would tear and disappear. The clouds would come back in shapes of animals and angels – in any form Clarissa wanted to imagine. Sometimes she felt that she was moving too, travelling in the sky without her body. One day when there were no clouds, she had imagined the earth turning upside down and landing her in a bright blue bowl of sky she could never climb out of. She had closed her eyes against the frightening thought.

Clarissa hated arithmetic. She could never figure out numbers. As soon as Miss Ellis put a sum on the board, Clarissa's day was ruined. When the school ma'am tried to explain multiplication and fractions one day, Clarissa laughed.

"You are setting a bad example, Clarissa," said Miss Ellis in a hard voice. "Learning must be taken seriously. When you go to the shop you need to know how to add and subtract money, and when you bake a cake in the school kitchen you must know your fractions. Imagine putting in a cup of soda powders when you need only half a cup."

Clarissa almost giggled, imagining Miss Ellis taking a mouthful of cake that had a cup – or even half a cup – of soda powders in it.

Cora had put up her hand to correct Miss Ellis. The school ma'am seemed pleased. "I'm glad some of you are on your toes and have learned from our Home Economics classes that soda powders must be used sparingly."

Clarissa liked the Home Economics classes the school ma'am had started. They took place once a week in the school's tiny kitchen. On those days, she sneaked a spoonful of powdered Klim milk – and then another. That satisfied her hunger on some of the mornings when she couldn't stomach porridge.

Once school ended for the day, the children walked quietly to the door, but as soon as they were outside they rushed down the steps, their pent-up voices let loose. Clarissa moved slowly, her body needing time to come back to life after a long time sitting. She was not allowed to undo the straps and loosen her braces during class. The brace strapping her right leg from her hip to her ankle sometimes cut into her leg. After a while, it was as if pins and needles were stabbing it. The short brace on the other leg made it fidgety.

Ida, the merchant's daughter, whispered to her friends as they passed Clarissa, "God bless the mark." It was spoken loud enough for Clarissa to hear. She wished that Ida's tongue was in a brace. Some people were superstitious enough to believe that when they passed someone who was disfigured or lame they should say "God bless the mark" so that nothing like that would happen to them.

Cora surprised Clarissa by slowing down to wait for her. She hadn't liked it that Clarissa had gone to bed in another dormitory without telling her until yesterday that she had been moved – and for good.

"The mistresses do what they like," Clarissa tried to tell her now. "I'm glad you brought my treasures."

Cora looked at her as if to retort. The girls turned at the sound of pounding hoofs. The children ahead of them screamed and dashed across the road, jumping the ditch and skittering behind the church. Cora was gone in a blink; Clarissa stared at the black bull charging towards her. She wanted to move out of its path; instead, she stopped still, the top of her head feeling as if it would explode with fright. She braced herself on her crutches, her eyes meeting the bull's red, sore-looking ones as it got nearer. Her eyes closed and she stood trembling, waiting for the awful strength of the bull to hit her body, flattening her, suffocating her – killing her! And with all the bad thoughts she had against other people, she couldn't be sure she was going to Heaven.

"Clarissa – Clarissa!" Cora's voice dragged at her. Finally she opened her eyes. The bull was nowhere in sight. She turned her head quickly, alarmed that it might hook her from behind. But it was going on down the road. She stood for a moment, her smooth forehead furrowing. The bull had gone past her as if she was nothing more than a speck of dirt.

All of a sudden she felt vexed that the other children ran away without caring what happened to her. She staggered on to the orphanage, her jaw set. She wouldn't talk to any of them for the rest of the day, especially Cora.

Cora ran to catch up, calling, "I'm sorry Clarissa. I couldn't stop a bull from running over you if I tried – and I'm too scared of bulls not to run. One time, a bull hooked my arm." She lifted her coat sleeve, baring her right arm. A scar ran down it like a rivulet of water down a windowpane.

Clarissa had noticed the scar before, but she had never asked about it. Her lips softened. "Oh, it's all right, fraidy-cat." Still, she swung herself to the orphanage in silence.

Clarissa was afraid of the husky dog team Dr. Grenfell had given the older boys for training, afraid that their yawping would lead to biting. Once, she had gotten too close to a har-bour man's husky. It had snapped at her crutches, knocking her to the ground before the owner whipped the dog away from her. Dogs and bulls! One lot could tear you to pieces; the other could stomp you to death. She didn't know which one was scarier.

8
WINTER

One morning while Clarissa was dressing, she glanced at the dormitory window and her brown eyes widened in delight at the sight of a bunch of exquisite ferns, horses' manes and tree leaves caught in silvery etchings on the long window-pane. She hobbled to the window, leaned forward, and blew a hole in Jack Frost's silver curtain. Usually winter came running into the harbour like a growling husky, backing residents indoors for fear of its snarling bite. This year it had come gently, quietly rubbing away autumn's fading hold on the land. The silence of the harbour under the thin spread of frozen water drifted into Clarissa's senses. Dr. Grenfell's little medical ship, the *Strathcona,* sat in the sheltered harbour caught in ice, waves of snow around it. She stared at the white mass of ocean, imagining she could go beyond this place – walk on solid water to her home.

The other girls were just getting into their clothes, stunned and sleepy looks on their faces, as Clarissa pushed open the door and went out. She hurried down the stairs and moved as quietly as she could through the hall and past the dining room so she could be on the orphanage steps before anyone else. She dragged her red coat and cap from her locker, pulling them on as she sat on a stool. Her mittened hands inside their sealskin cuffs grabbed for her crutches and she swung her way to the door. Outside, she paused on the steps, glad the wind she'd heard whistling through the night had dropped to a whisper. Winter had settled itself over a sleeping earth like an angora blanket below the moon, a crystal coin still hanging in the sky. *Every building, every fence, and every black dog – if it stays still – will have a fluffy white coat,* she thought joyfully. Soon the harbour children would be randying down a snow-packed Fox Farm Hill.

A few light snowflakes fell like stars on Clarissa's long red coat as she made her way carefully down the steps, leaving behind the smudged prints of her crutches and gaiters. The movement of her feet and crutches spun the light snow into the air. She let herself slip slowly down into its soft, magical world, rolling over and over in it until she was tired. Then she spread her arms, arcing them back and forth. She moved her legs as far as they would go without feeling pain. There used to be lots of pain whenever the physical therapist had forced her legs into exercise years ago.

Soon all the children would be out, falling around in the fine snow, trying to make snowballs. But for now she was alone and content, not caring that the orphan boys would soon be complaining about having to haul her to school on a sled.

"Clarissa!" The harsh sound of her name hit her ears like a whip swishing through the air. She turned to meet Miss Elizabeth's nettled look. The woman was looking down at her from the top of the steps. "You get up from the snow this minute. There's no time for childish games. You're without your canvas dickey and you've dampened your clothes. That makes for a chill on your way to school. You missed your breakfast. You know what that means."

Clarissa looked towards Miss Elizabeth, feeling slightly foolish. The other children were tumbling out the door, and looking her way. Cora hurried down to her friend. "I've got your bookbag and your lunch in it," she said. Then she whispered, "Did you have fun?" Clarissa grinned up at her. She settled her face as Jakot walked by, his big, round face looking like it had two black bull's eyes in it, and her red coat was a red flag.

Soon he was pulling a sled from the barn, its rusted runners making brown marks through the clean, white snow. He stopped and glared at Clarissa as she got up from the ground. "Here comes the cripple," he muttered to the other boys. They laughed as if she couldn't even hear them, as if she was deaf as well as crippled. *There's nothing wrong with my tongue*, she thought, *and I'll give you all a lash with it if you don't leave me alone.*

Peter came up beside the sled, his face long. He knew he would have to take his turn hauling Clarissa. "It's bad enough to have to tramp through the snow ourselves," he grumbled. "You could walk on your feet if you tried hard enough." He pushed her and she fell down on the sled.

Jakot turned his back and started to pull Clarissa. She hurried to straighten herself on the sled. "You'll not tag Clarissa a cripple," Missus Frances called from the orphanage steps. "She is much more than her limbs and their posture, just as you are much more than your sometimes very bad dispositions. Some of you boys are so lazy," she muttered, "you would be happy to be a sled in summer and a wheelbarrow in winter."

Clarissa ignored the boys, keeping to her own thoughts.

She daydreamed of running – and flying, her legs like wings, lifting her above the likes of mean boys – and girls.

"You're not my sister or my brother. I don't know why I have to pull you," Jakot complained. He grunted and gave the sled a jerk. Clarissa's head popped back. Owen, Cora's ruddy-faced brother, ran up beside Jakot and took Clarissa's crutches. He would take his turn pulling once they got over the first hill. Whenever he pulled Clarissa, he did it with patience, and he was nice to her.

The children walking ahead looked like moving cut-outs going up the steep tolt to the school. They disappeared inside long before Clarissa's sled got there. Snow clung to the corners of the school windows like angels' hair. Twig-like marks multiplied as little birds dropped to the soft surface of new snow. Clarissa watched a thin cat, hunched on a fence post, leap into an emptiness left by a snowbird beating the air to grab its freedom. A feather drifted past the cat's nose.

* * *

Clarissa forgot about the hungry cat as she sat in school. All morning she was afraid her empty stomach would rumble. She was glad when lunchtime came. She took the slice of buttered bread from her bookbag; Cora's mother always put one slice of buttered bread in each child's bag. Clarissa and Cora toasted their bread on the red-hot pot-bellied stove, coughing as the hot butter smoked the air. Clarissa finished her lunch still hungry; one cut of cobbler's bread was only a teaser. She followed Cora out to the porch and dipped her enamel cup into a bucket of water, and lifted it full to the brim. She drank quickly. Then she went to the bucket for a second cup, hoping a bellyful of water would keep her from feeling hungry. She looked at Cora. "By the time we get back to the orphanage, we'll be hungry enough to faint twice over, and there'll be no supper for me."

"I know." Cora shook her head. "I wish Momma could give yer food, but she can't – not against Missus Frances's orders." The girls followed the other children to their places as Miss Ellis called lunchtime to a close with the ringing of her bell. The school ma'am's look ran around the room before it dug into Clarissa. "You will come up to my desk and read your language assignment: a description of an animal you would like to be," she said briskly.

Clarissa leaned on her crutches and went forward. When she reached the school ma'am's desk, she looked at the class. And then she lowered her head to read from her scribbler: "I would not wish to be anything but human," she began. "Animals have a greater chance of being killed and eaten. But if I were to be an animal, I would be one that was not there in the beginning of the world to get its name. Everyone would look at me and someone would ask, 'What kind of animal is that?' No one would be able to guess, because I was created in mystery. I would look like the most beautiful dog who ever lived. My fur would be blue and shine like diamonds. I would not bark or speak. Whenever I came close to anyone who was sick, they would feel better. They would be happy and smile. My thoughts would float into people's ears like music they could listen to all day. No one could ever hurt me. I would run fast, and when I wanted to, I would fly in the sky like an eagle. I would never be hungry." Clarissa looked at Miss Ellis and smiled. Her smile faded as the boys began to snigger. Miss Ellis silenced them with a sharp look.

As Clarissa moved past the school ma'am, her right crutch struck Miss Ellis's foot. Clarissa tripped and hit an ink bottle on the desk; it struck the edge and tipped into the woman's lap. Clarissa couldn't take her eyes off the blue stain creeping over the school ma'am's mauve dress, its beautiful white collar and cuffs now flecked. She couldn't help thinking: *What a lot of interesting words that bottle of ink could have made, instead of a blotch and dots that scream, "You're clumsy!"*

Clarissa's eyes and the school ma'am's lifted from the spreading ink at the same time. Pupil and teacher faced each other; Miss Ellis pursed her lips and a black hair on her chin lifted like a wire. Clarissa tried to look sorry, though she didn't know why she had to be sorry for something that was an accident.

"Up in the corner!" the school ma'am ordered her in a voice that seemed strong enough to pick her up and put her there. A few minutes earlier, Peter had kicked the desk irons, and the school ma'am had ordered him into the corner. Now she asked for his dunce cap. He passed it to her with a saucy grin and Miss Ellis lowered it onto Clarissa's head. "There you go, off to the corner."

Clarissa smiled broadly at the thought of having crutches at one end and a dunce cap at the other.

The school ma'am dabbed at her dress with a cloth she kept in her desk. Then she looked at the class, her eyelids drooping over her eyes. "One thing about Clarissa," she said, "you can punish her one minute, but she's smiling the next."

Clarissa decided to spend her corner time using her imagination. She began to write a story in her mind for Treffie, imagining that it was the sky she was facing and not a dreary old corner. *Clouds are made from angels' hair. When angels clean their hairbrushes, the hair falls into the sky.*

Young angels have dark hair and older angels have white hair. That's why there are light and dark clouds. Sometimes the sun comes out and burns up the clouds. Then another bunch of hair falls from an angel's brush. Angels never go bald and they never die. That is why we will always have clouds.

After Miss Ellis let Clarissa return to her place, she copied down her story for Treffie. The school ma'am came down, picked it up and read it with her nose in the air. "You're not short on imagination, but imagination can be a deceitful thing," she warned her. "It can make a person believe things that aren't true."

"But it's only a story I wrote for Treffie because she has angel's hair," Clarissa said earnestly.

"Hmm . . . the new orphan. In that case," said Miss Ellis, "I will give you an adequate mark."

Once school was dismissed for the day and the children hurried outside, boys who usually ran on ahead lagged behind laughing. One harbour boy taunted her. "So you want to be a blue furry animal, do yer now? 'Tis der school ma'am's skin dat's blue. T'anks ter you."

Clarissa leaned against the school and took her scribbler out of her bookbag. She tore its pages to pieces, scattering her stories into the air. The wind lifted them for a moment, and then they fell like snowflakes to the ground. "See if I'll write anything like that again," she muttered.

Jakot stood jiggling one skin-booted leg beside the sled. Clarissa settled down on it without a word. She passed her crutches to Peter who sometimes carried them; other times he let them hobble over the snow. Today, he lifted them to push the sled. Once he jabbed Clarissa's back and she let out a sharp cry. It mingled with bully boy's laugh. When they got to the top of the first hill, Jakot let go of the sled. Clarissa sat rigid with fear as the sled picked up speed; her eyes widened in horror at the sight of a tree straight ahead. She swung herself to one side and went head over heels into a snowbank. Blood dripped into the snow from where a tooth had cut into her tongue and lip.

Jakot laughed. "That's how to get her partway from school."

"You big blubber-eater, Jakot – you Eskimo Plague!" shouted Owen as he helped Clarissa up and back on the sled. "I ought to give yer face the turn of me hand. You could have killed Clarissa. A fine fix you'd be in then."

Peter came up beside them, and laughed scornfully. "'Tis no more than you'd expect from someone whose people drinks girls' pee to make 'em strong, and lifts the skins on the bottom of their igloos to use toilet holes made in the ice."

Jakot backed away from the boys ganging up on him. "I didn't mean ter let her go," he whined. "The rope slipped from me cuff."

Clarissa felt a surge of pity. She had to put up with the Eskimo, and he had to put up with other boys calling him The Eskimo Plague and playing tricks on him. A scar on his lip stood out raw white in the cold air. It was a reminder of when he was younger, and one of the older orphans had tricked him into putting his sloppy mouth on a cold metal bar; his lips had frozen onto the bar. His flesh had torn when he tried to get away.

Peter pulled Clarissa, with jerks and stops, until he had her inside the orphanage gates. Then he tipped the sled over and Clarissa fell into the snow. Owen dropped her crutches beside her. She lifted them slowly, knowing there was no reason for her to rush to get inside the orphanage. She had to go to bed without supper. *I'm so hungry, I can almost swallow my tongue for food,* she thought as she started up the steps. The other children rushed ahead of her, even Cora.

Clarissa hadn't meant to go outside without having her breakfast. She had been drawn to the beauty of the snow, new and unmarked. Now she would go hungry as punishment. Whenever she was late for breakfast and didn't get supper, the night stretched before her like a long journey she dreaded.

As soon as she reached the inside of the orphanage, Miss Elizabeth spoke, "Get up the stairs!"

It was no good for Clarissa to put on a long face. So many times she had struggled to get home from school, knowing it was useless to rush. Though she was feeling famished there would be no supper for her.

She looked up at the layers of steps she had to climb to be in a dormitory for hours by herself. She stopped to beg. "I only wanted to have fun in the snow."

"There are rules to abide by," the mistress replied in a sharp voice, putting out her hand and pushing Clarissa towards the stairs. She lost her balance, and fell on the floor to the clatter of her braces and crutches.

"You are letting your stubbornness overcome your sense," the mistress added, her brown eyes threatening. "I'm going to the kitchen to get a stick. That will knock the Irish sulk out of you."

As Clarissa was getting to her feet, she saw the mistress coming back with the rod. *Old Keziah can beat the black man out of me. I'm not going upstairs and I'm not all Irish,* she thought angrily. *Missus Frances told me I have French blood from my mother's side, mixed with the English and Irish blood from my father.*

Miss Elizabeth held the stick and frowned at Clarissa. "I won't let you go to the next birthday party if you don't get up the stairs now."

The next birthday party would be for her and Peter in January. Last year, when she had untied the parcel holding her mother's birthday gift, she'd found a tiny slide projector with built-in slides of children and animals. She took the projector out of her treasure bag only when she was alone, for fear someone would take it. One day she left it on the bed; when she came back to the dormitory, it had disappeared. The other girls denied seeing it.

Clarissa started up the stairs, passing the lantern that stayed lit in the hall at night, and went into the dark room, wishing for a piece of hard tack. She got ready for bed, and slid under the warm counterpane. She soon drifted past her hunger into a sound sleep.

She awoke startled. For a moment she thought she was back at the hospital and rats were gnawing on the walls. It was only the other girls munching on hard tack. Every second suppertime, Ilish brought out a pan holding cakes of hard tack halved and buttered, ready for the children to take to their dormitories. The sound of the other girls filling their bellies was enough to make Clarissa want to be good, though she often wondered what it was about her that was so bad.

She was falling back to sleep when a beam of light touched her eyelids. Miss Elizabeth was standing by her bed holding a lamp. "Now Clarissa," she said, loud enough for the other girls to hear, "be sure to use the lobby before you go to sleep. You know what can happen."

It had not happened for a long time and Old Keziah's words shamed her. Besides, all the water must be drained out of her. She hadn't had a drink since lunch. She held herself tight as she lay in bed, feeling mortified that the other girls knew she had wet her bed when she was on the lower floor.

That night she dreamed of a pretty young woman in a white gown, her hair braided around her head. She floated above a wild sea with her hands outstretched. Clarissa reached her hands as far as she could, even her weak left one, hoping to have her small hands clasped in the hands of the woman she knew must be her mother. She strained and strained, but her fingertips could not reach her mother's. Tears filled the woman's eyes and spilled down a face that stayed as still as if it were carved out of wood, like the face of the statue of the Blessed Madonna. The tears dripped into the sea and mingled with it. "You have beautiful hands, Mommy," Clarissa said. But it was as if she had not spoken. Her mother did not answer. Then she drifted away into a black fog.

In the morning when Clarissa woke up, she fancied she could see herself being lifted into a large boat while her mother cried. She tried to bring the image close, but it stayed veiled – unreal. Something appeared real. A string of beads linked to a tiny cross had hung from her mother's wrist: the same string of beads she had in her treasure bag. Housemother Simmons had seen Clarissa playing with the beads. She told her: "These are not for playing with; they are beads Catholics say prayers on, prayers to Mary, the Mother of God. Protestants don't need beads to speak to God." She raised an eyebrow, her mouth set.

Clarissa got her treasure bag and poured the beads out into her hand. She tightened her fingers over the cross on her palm for a moment before she put the beads back in the bag. Then she sat pondering her past. She knew there had to be a reason why she was kept at the orphanage. Perhaps Dr. Grenfell knew what it was. Maybe it was *his* secret. A dark question mark made sickle swipes inside her mind.

9

WAITING FOR CHRISTMAS

" *A few more days of the blistering voices of grownups splashing vinegar into the cuts of children's lives and it will be Christmas.*" Clarissa looked up from the pages of *Just Looking At You,* and the complaint of the book's forlorn heroine. "That sounds like this orphanage," she muttered.

Clarissa loved Christmas, not only because of the gifts, but because it came with a glad spirit that moved through the orphanage, touching even the mistresses and making them laugh.

The Saturday before Christmas, Clarissa and Cora were on their way to their dormitories when they heard voices coming from the Grenfell shop on the first floor. Clarissa sneaked along the hall slowly, trying to avoid tapping her crutches too loudly on the wooden floor. The door to the shop was open a few inches, and the girls could see barrels of clothes and goods that had been gathered from the kind people of the United States and Canada and shipped to St. Anthony weeks ago. Miss Elizabeth's and Missus Frances's heads were down in the barrels; they were busy pulling out tuck-away gifts for the children. "We had better not let them see us, or we'll get nothing,"

Cora cautioned Clarissa. She slid quietly past the door and up the stairs to go to her dormitory. Clarissa followed, her brown eyes alight with the anticipation of a Christmas surprise that would not come from Canada or the United States – or even the North Pole.

The girls stopped at a window near the stairwell, both of them wrapped in thoughts of Christmas gifts. Outside, in the dusky afternoon, a light shimmered up from the harbour. "'Tis a glim – a reflection the ice throws off on its way to shore," Clarissa had overheard Uncle Aubrey tell Miss Elizabeth as they stood on the orphanage steps last week. Now the bay lay silent under ice thickened into a seascape, as residents explored the large surface on foot and on sleds pulled by huskies, their cacophony and breath rising in the dry, empty sky.

Like walking on water, Clarissa thought as she watched Dr. Grenfell running across an area of ice now used as a football field. The dapper-looking doctor often showed up unexpectedly, arriving over the hills on a dogsled, or walking down from his home to tumble with the boys in the snow. He beckoned for the lads, as he called them, to come play football with him. A cap rose in the air and came down on its crown. Peter got to be captain of one team and Jakot of the other. They set up josh posts in the ice and picked their players without arguing, but only because of the doctor's presence. He always took turns playing with each side, kicking the ball, a pig's bladder, as vigorously as any of the boys. Afterwards he would always declare, "It was all jolly good fun." Sometimes the doctor set up obstacle courses on the ice, and included the girls in the game – all the girls except Clarissa.

She shifted her gaze from the window to look at Cora, but her friend had gone. When Clarissa turned back to the window, she saw her running across the ice. The window was open a crack, and she could hear Cora calling to Ettie and Becky.

Clarissa took her time getting downstairs. She hauled on her coat and mitts and went outside. She sat on the cold orphanage steps all day, yearning to be able to hit or toss a ball. Peter passed her after the game had finished. He taunted, "You're deformed!"

"You're misinformed," she shouted at him.

He looked back at her with a puzzled look. She knew he was wondering if the word *misinformed* had as terrible a meaning as *deformed*.

* * *

At the dining room table the next morning, Treffie coughed as if her insides were going to rip open and scatter her heart and everything else around the room. Miss Elizabeth came and stood over her. "Your handkerchief, Trophenia. Put it to your mouth. When you cough like that, your breath can be dragged into the nostrils of anyone near you. Then they will be coughing it back out like you are doing. We don't want that, do we?"

Treffie looked at Miss Elizabeth, her eyes wet and drawn; she didn't answer.

"Take your elbows off the table, Trophenia," the mistress said, tilting her head towards the little girl. Treffie jerked her arms away so quickly her glass tipped over, spilling water over the table. Her shoulders began to shake, and her little hands shot up to cover her face.

"We allow for accidents," the mistress said in a voice as hard as a stick, "but in future, Trophenia, don't act so hastily, and do not have the same accidents, or we will consider them bad habits that need to be broken. Rules," the mistress added, "are to be enforced. See this wooden ruler?" She held up a heavy, thick stick. "Does it bend? No, it does not. Does it have measurements on it? Most certainly. And that is why punishment for infractions vary."

Clarissa sighed, but not loud enough for Old Keziah to hear her. The mistress liked to answer her own questions while the children stared at her, some of them with eyes so round and protruding Miss Elizabeth could almost knock them out of their heads with one swipe of her ruler.

Most of the children had learned that, although the mistresses were against bending the rules, they didn't mind bending a ruler on someone's behind.

10

DISAPPOINTMENT AT CHRISTMAS

The eve of Christmas slipped in through a dark morning and opened up into a crystal-white day. The scent of Christmases past seemed to waft against Clarissa's nose; the gaiety of the season came like a red candle, its flame a dancing ballerina. She felt her insides liven in the shining hope of Christmas. *Even miserable Miss Elizabeth is going to enjoy Christmas; she won't be able to help herself,* Clarissa thought as she made her way to the dining room.

"Chew, chew, don't talk." Today Miss Elizabeth's voice was gentle as she came into the dining room, where the children's whispers had burst into chatter. The children looked towards her as her thin lips opened into a smile – a Christmas surprise.

Later, when the children were dismissed, they scattered into the hall. The mistress's pleasant look disappeared into a frown at the sight of what she called highjinking conduct by boys wrestling on the floor. She tutted, "You boys are bent on hurling the Christmas spirit out the window." Afraid that the dreaded words "no lunch and no supper" would fall on their ears, the boys got up and scampered up the stairs.

Still, Christmas is the best of times, even better than birth-days, because a glad spirit is in so many people at the same time, Clarissa thought as she stood on the orphanage steps after lunch. *Everyone's thoughts are strung together in the hope of getting a Christmas box that will make them forget all the bad things that ever happened to them.* She would be able to forget the housemothers and mistresses' scoldings, the orphans' taunts, her uncertainty about ever leaving the orphan-age, if there was a present from her real family. Her heart som-ersaulted in anticipation.

From where she was standing, Clarissa could see the Grenfell Hospital. Against its front walls, on packed snow, har-bour dogs lay with their tails curled over their noses. The dogs looked up at the windows, now and then, as if searching for a familiar face and a treat. A guarded look crossed their faces and their ears stood up straight when they heard the squeals of chil-dren and the howls of huskies mingling in the afternoon air. They knew what would happen to them if a temperamental husky got loose from its traces.

Dr. Grenfell had given the orphanage boys a husky dog team. Now Jakot, Peter and other older boys were on their way up Fox Farm Hill to cut a tree and greens to decorate the orphanage. The huskies bristled and lifted their heads, howl-ing like wolves as they pulled the sleds past barking harbour dogs. Jakot, the driver, swung his whip through the air, making it whistle like a strong wind. He bragged that one day he would be as good as his Uncle Joe. The old trapper could whisk the button off a coat, or knock a cigar from someone's mouth with his fifty-four-foot whip.

Clarissa moved out by the gates to listen to the shouts of children and the yapping of dogs. Today she felt peace among the noises.

When the supper bell rang, she followed the rest of the children indoors. She stopped to watch Caleb Rose, who was as meek and as mild a boy as any mistress could want, painting Santa Claus in water colours on the dining room wall. He was finishing the tip of one of Santa's black boots, about to touch down on a red brick chimney. Clarissa made her way to her seat, feeling a delightful shudder, even though she likened Santa Claus to fairies.

"Let us say our prayers," Miss Elizabeth called, watching to see that her charges closed their eyes. The children mouthed Christmas prayers for the coming of the Christ Child, and then ate quickly. The younger children were eager to go to bed and settle down to sleep as fast as they could, so that Christmas morning would come more quickly.

The mistress clapped her hands and dismissed the children. "Off to bed with you now, you younger boys and girls. Do not make a squeak," she warned. "You are in bed to sleep and to grow up while you are doing it."

"I'll shove off to bed, I will, too, Miss," Peter piped up, a mischievous look in his eyes, "if you'll answer a riddle."

"A riddle! Very well, seeing it is Christmas," Miss Elizabeth answered tolerantly. "A scrap of lenience for levity, if you will be brief."

Peter grinned and recited: "Four legs up cold as stone / Two legs down, flesh and bone / The head of the living in the mouth of the dead / Tell me the riddle and I'll go to bed."

Everyone laughed, and one of the orphans shouted, "I know – I know the answer!"

Peter said, "Whist!" with his finger to the side of his mouth, a habit of Housemother Simmons's. But Ben, a young boy who had a tight little face, a harelip and dark, sad eyes under blond hair, called out, "A man walking with a bark pot on his head, Miss."

Peter looked sullen. "'Tis the mistress I wanted to answer."

The mistress's eyebrows lifted. "Come on with it, then. What is the real answer? A bark pot? What is that?"

Peter crinkled his nose and replied, "Young Ben gave the answer. A bark pot has four legs and is used to soak fishermen's sails and nets in tree bark and buds to keep them. And you thinks we're the ignorant ones. We knows what we knows, and you knows what you knows. I think meself, Miss, that makes us equal."

The mistress looked at him as if she wanted to set his eyes afloat in soapy water. Instead, she said in a tight voice, "Off with you now."

The young orphans were shooed up to bed. House helpers trailed behind, making sure the children went straight to their own dormitories. They ran off shouting riddles to each other.

"What grows with its roots up?" called Ben.

The other orphans chanted, "Conkerbell! Conkerbell! Jack Frost hangs it from the roof. When it hits the ground, it rings."

Clarissa stopped to look at Caleb's painting of Santa. She had never seen a smiling Santa before; this one had a gold tooth, like the one Missus Frances had but rarely showed. Clarissa smiled back at Santa. Then she trailed the other girls, who were just starting up the stairs. Missus Frances called out, "Come into the parlour, Girls." They all turned towards her, eager to get inside the staff's living quarters.

Clarissa had been only as far as the lounge. Now the girls followed Missus Frances through the lounge to a cosy little room. Clarissa once heard the older girls talking about the time Dr. Grenfell had asked them into the room. He sat in a big, green armchair, having a cup of tea from a small teapot that Missus Frances had placed on a little gate-leg table covered in a white lace cloth. He had leaned forward with his cup, and told the girls about his grave ordeal on the ocean. He said he would never forget what happened after he set out with his dog team across a frozen bay to visit a patient. The wind changed, setting him adrift on a small pan of ice with his dogs; he had to sacrifice three of them to save himself and the other dogs. Clarissa's stomach turned over at the thought that if Dr. Grenfell had died, she would not have had a doctor to help her walk – even with the help of crutches.

"Your mind, Clarissa, where has it taken off to now?" the mistress asked.

"It's right here inside my head," she answered and sat down quickly.

When the girls were seated, the mistress began to read the younger orphans' letters to Santa. Clarissa listened to their dreams: a new pair of boots, a doll, a wind-up truck, a cat . . . their own mothers and fathers.

"We can try to make your dreams come true, except for wishes to have parents and live animals," the mistress told them. She added, with a twist to her lips, "A cat would not last too long around here with all the dogs." She took pencils from a metal cup on the mantel and pulled sheets of paper from the tablet she held in her hands, passing one to each girl. "Here, write your wishes."

Clarissa looked at her and said softly, "My wish is to go home – and I'll go someday." Her words tightened over the promise to herself, her body trembling with anticipation. The mistress lifted her eyebrows. "You seem contented here."

"That's because my mind doesn't put everything I think on my tongue," Clarissa answered.

"I dare say 'tis many a sigh you'll make before that day," Celetta said with a satisfied look on her face.

"I will go home," Clarissa answered in a stubborn voice, "and I will get well and have two good legs and strong arms and no more pain in my limbs." She lowered her head, and bit her lip to keep the tears inside.

Imogene rolled her eyes. The other girls pretended not to have heard as they wrote their wishes in front of the hearth where fire leaped and danced above wood crackling in the large grate. A flanker popped out on the stone shelf and Cora exclaimed, "Strangers are coming!"

"A superstition, my dear," chided the mistress, "but someone *is* coming, and he is no stranger to the minds of children. It is time to take your letters, and toss them into the fireplace." Missus Frances's smile widened enough to show her gold tooth. She lifted her arms into the air. "Now!"

As quick as a wink, everyone tossed their letters into the fire. "Close your eyes," the mistress added. "Now imagine the wings of the fire sending all the wishes up through the chimney out into the night. They shall fly on the wind through the sky and into Santa's castle at the North Pole."

"Well, I don't know, I'm sure," said Imogene. She had flung her letter with an uppity tilt to her nose, and kept her eyes open long enough to see the letters burn to ashes in the grate. "'Tis a little late to be choosing presents with Santa already in the skies. Sure, if he's on his way, he's on his way with whatever is already in his sleigh."

"That's the magic of it, " Missus Frances said quickly, rising from her chair. "Off with you now; the dining room needs decorating. No beds for you, yet!"

The older orphan boys were coming from a gymnastic round in the playroom as the girls were leaving the mistresses' quarters. "What is it you're about in there?" asked Jakot, his lip turned up to his nose. The girls pretended they hadn't heard him. They went inside the dining room to decorate the boughs Jakot and other boys had left there, already bent with wire into wreaths. The pleasure of helping make Christmas happen surged through Clarissa as she helped trim the wreaths with bows of red ribbons. The girls put red tissue handkerchiefs on each bough of the Christmas tree, tucking them around green candles.

Clarissa and Cora were shaping stars from lead foil saved from pounds of tea and kept in an old tea chest, when they caught each other's eye. Clarissa knew Cora was thinking the same thing she was: that the box on Tea House Hill would be buried in snow sweeping in through the loose boards of the Tea House. It would be buried too deep for anyone to find and open. Clarissa crossed her fingers and made a wish: *let the box be there next summer for us to open.*

After the girls finished decorating the dining room, Miss Elizabeth called them upstairs. "Now, Girls, it is time to make the candy bags for that special Christmas treat. Ilish is cutting out squares of gauze. She will help you."

The girls followed the mistress to the sewing room on the second floor. Ilish's round face was flushed with excitement as she passed the girls blocks of gauze, needles and thread. They busied themselves sewing bags for the candy they and the younger children would receive. Imogene and Cora were getting on better than usual, tittering as if tickled by their own cute remarks. Clarissa was trying not to worry about Treffie in bed with a cold caught up on her chest. She was glad Treffie didn't have to go to the hospital. Her heart begged, *Please God, don't let Treffie be too sick to see the wreaths tied with red bows on the windows.*

It was just as well that Cora and Suzy were enjoying this Christmas. They both had a rattle on their chests. Cora didn't spend much time with her little sister because the two were in different dormitories; Suzy had made friends among the younger children. Clarissa glanced at Cora's happy face. She hoped it was influenza that Cora and her sister had, not consumption. Sometimes their colds cleared and they seemed almost healthy. Once the sisters got consumption, it would likely get rid of them, instead of them getting rid of it. Clarissa tried not to think about it as the girls finished stitching the bags. They piled them together before they left the room.

"Look, there's a star in front of the moon, the sign of civil weather for Santa's reindeer," Celetta called to the other girls as they entered the dormitory. The girls rushed to the window, getting there just as Housemother Simmons tapped on the door, calling to them to wash up and get to bed.

Clarissa lay in bed with the blankets pulled up to her chin, seeing the moon as a silver ornament hung in the sky. Christmas Eve was like a breath held in all over the world. She imagined reindeer, foxes and bears in the woods dropping to their knees at the stroke of midnight in honor of Jesus's birthday. Maybe even husky dogs would kneel in their kennels. The wonder of Christmas made Clarissa's fingers and toes tingle. Her gaze stayed on the window: any time now, she might see the hooves of Santa's reindeer. *There's no point in having an imagination if you can't use it*, she thought. A cloud – or maybe Santa and his sleigh – crossed the moon, and darkness covered the window, filling the room and settling against her face like dark velvet. She fell asleep thinking of Christmas Day as a gift-wrapped box, its string ready to be burst and Christmas unwrapped.

It seemed that she had just fallen asleep when she woke up

to a rustle in the dormitory. Her eyelashes lifted enough for her
to see what had awakened her. Miss Elizabeth stood in the doorway holding a lamp while Missus Frances tiptoed to each bed,
laying a Christmas stocking on the foot of it. Clarissa didn't wonder why Missus Frances was in the room and not Santa. Santa
was only as real as her imagination; she closed her eyes and pretended it was Santa who was leaving the stockings.

Clarissa drifted back to sleep and dreamed that Santa had
brought her a stocking full of reindeer turds. She stirred to the
clanging of the bell as the dark drifts of night disappeared.
There was a sudden clatter of voices in the hall. Some children
were already on their way downstairs.

Clarissa sat on her bed and lifted her Christmas stocking.
Inside were an orange, an apple and some peanuts. She pulled
out the orange wrapped in a tissue handkerchief and bit into it
to pull off the rind; orange zest sprayed the cold air. Its scent
mingled with the cool sweet scent of the apple. She knew the
apple would have the star of Bethlehem in its centre. She
would eat it and the peanuts later.

Becky came into the bath and toilet room while Clarissa
was brushing her teeth. "I saw Missus Frances put the
Christmas stockings on our beds," she said, sounding disappointed.

Clarissa shrugged. "You can't expect Santa to fill stockings
and do everything else. Besides, where would *he* get apples
and oranges – and peanuts? He can't grow fruit and peanuts at
the North Pole. You'll get a Christmas box downstairs."

Becky's freckled face relaxed and she went off to catch up
with Imogene and the other girls, who had already left to go
downstairs. Clarissa was left alone to take her time. She could
hear the strains of the children's favourite carol, "Away in a
Manger," from the Victrola as she made her way slowly down

the steps. Someone was playing an accordion, too, but the sound was nothing more than a cough and a wheeze.

Most of the older children were in the hall when Clarissa got there. She accepted her slice of buttered bread for breakfast and waited for the dining room doors to open.

There were gasps as one child after another rushed into the dining room. They stopped to stare at a tree dressed in red bows, green candles and silver stars. Gauze bags of hard candy were piled against its base. There was not a present in sight – just an empty wooden cot on rockers beside the tree.

"No presents! 'Tis just like when the world was in war, and four of the harbour's fellows went off to fight," Peter exclaimed.

"That's okay," Cora said. "'Tis fewer bad people in the world now because the good people killed them. Sure, that's a Christmas gift."

Imogene spoke up, lifting her tight, little chin to gain attention. "There could be lots of reasons why Santa didn't come. His suit could have caught on fire last year when he came down the chimney, and he was left with nothing to wear. Maybe there were too many children in the poor countries who needed regarding, or – " her voice dropped to a whisper, "Santa could have just up and died."

The younger children looked at her with horrified faces before turning back to the tree. They were still staring at it, when Miss Elizabeth swept into the room in a navy dress with a square collar as white as new snow. The children didn't seem to notice she was holding a white bundle until she announced, "We are celebrating the good tide of Christmas knowing we are a privileged lot. Many children in the harbour didn't get their stockings filled. Most of them are thankful just to have stockings to put their feet in and a crust of bread and jam on their plates."

Clarissa thought of Esther. The image of the harbour girl, likely not much older than herself, drably dressed and grimy, was like a match put to a piece of coloured paper, burning to ashes what was left of her joyous emotions.

"Don't forget to thank God for Dr. Grenfell and the people around the world who help him keep you healthy and happy," the mistress said, her smile so wide that a dimple showed in one cheek. *It's not a dimple that God's fingertip pressed into her cheek,* Clarissa thought. *A dent is what it is, made by a smile her face wasn't ready for.*

"Yes, Miss Elizabeth." The children's voices rose in chorus, their heads bowed. "We thank God for the food we eat, and for the boots upon our feet. Father, we thank Thee."

The children's eyes widened as the mistress walked to the tree. She bent down to the wooden cot and laid the white bundle in it. "If the baby Jesus had not come, we would not have Christmas," she said gently. "This baby is a reminder that you are fortunate to have a home, and people in it who have become your family."

The children rushed to look at the pouty-faced baby, but Housemother Priddle, who took care of the younger children, shooed them away. "We don't want this motherless little child to catch the diseases that's around and about," she said with a firm lip. "He's under the tree to honour the baby Jesus."

The dining room door opened again, and an energetic young Ben galloped around the room on a hobby horse. Everyone was looking at the boy. They didn't see Santa Claus sneak in and stand right beside Treffie, who wouldn't be kept in bed on Christmas Day. When Treffie saw the black boots beside her, she looked up, wide-eyed, and let out a squeal. Her eyes closed and her body made a little shudder as she slid to the floor in front of the man in a Santa rig-out.

"Ho, Ho, Ho!" boomed a big voice Clarissa recognized as belonging to Dr. Curtis, an American who worked at the Grenfell Hospital. The big man scooped Treffie up in his arms and hurried to the tree with her. Her eyelashes flickered open and her eyes lit up as Santa put her down and grabbed up a bunch of candy bags. He passed a bag to Treffie. She looked up at him, her voice shaking. "I just took a little spell, Sir." Clutching her candy, she walked over and sat down beside Clarissa while Santa passed out the rest of the bags to the other children.

After the children sang "It came upon a Midnight Clear" with Missus Frances accompanying them on the piano, most of them scampered out into the hall. Clarissa and Cora stayed in the dining room. When Housemother Priddle went across the room to close a window, they hurried to get a close look at the baby.

Clarissa longed to lift the infant into her arms, to hold a beautiful, living doll for the first time. She knew that even if the housemother allowed her to pick him up, she wouldn't be able to hold him. He would slip from her arms, drop to the floor and get broken – maybe crippled. Then he would never get out of the orphanage.

Cora looked at the baby, her voice wistful. "I can't hold him because of my cough."

"And I can't hold him because of my infirmity," Clarissa said matter-of-factly.

Their chatter was stopped by the squawk of a tongue against their ears. "Out! Out! You young ones are not to be in here. Where is that wretched maid – housemother – whoever?" It was Miss Elizabeth in a fury, her arms beating the air as if the girls were flies she was trying to banish.

"We just wanted to look at the baby," Clarissa tried to

explain, knowing the woman's Christmas spirit must be on its way out already.

"Can we see the baby shortened?" Cora asked. "I've never seen a baby shortened."

"No, the child is a New Year's gift for some family. They'll have the joy of shortening him at three months. And the means to do it."

Clarissa imagined the party there would be on the day of the shortening. The baby, bundled up like a papoose since he was born, would finally get his legs loose. Dressed in booties, a knitted sweater, drawers and a cap, he would kick with all his might and blow bubbles in the face of anyone who pecked his cheek and cooed, "Coochy-coo."

I must have been shortened myself when I was a baby, Clarissa thought. *Maybe just in time to get a few kicks in before the ailment got at me.*

"Next you will want to lift him!" Miss Elizabeth shuddered. "You know what can come from being dropped."

"No, we don't," Cora whispered into Clarissa's ear as they hurried into the hall where children were squealing and laughing. Ben had found a present in his locker. A bright spin top was twirling on the floor. The other children ran to their lockers and lifted the covers; inside were gifts wrapped in green or red tissue paper. There were pocket combs, barrettes, knitted stockings, wooden spin tops, boats, harmonicas, a checkerboard, books – some with pictures. There were dolls made from bottles and dressed by Miss Pritcher, the seamstress. Boys who got push cars and tractors were soon truckling them across the hardwood floor.

Clarissa took what felt like a book from her locker, and was tearing the red tissue off when she saw, out of the corner of her eye, Missus Frances looking at her. The mistress crooked her finger and Clarissa laid down her gift and went towards the office, wondering what trouble she had gotten herself in now. Missus Frances closed the door and sat down. Clarissa stayed standing.

"You have another Christmas box, Clarissa, a white muff from your mother," the mistress informed her. Clarissa's heart leaped. Her family hadn't forgotten her.

The mistress shook her head. "It is quite impractical for you to wear a muff with your disability, even if there was no weakness in your left arm. We will keep it in the office. Besides, the other children will feel left out if they know you received an extra Christmas box. You cannot be selfish, Clarissa."

Clarissa stared at the mistress, wanting to beg for her muff, cry for it, knock the mistress to the floor with her crutches and search the big, wooden drawers in the office, but she knew there was nothing she could say or do to get her muff. Once the mistress set her mind, there was no changing it.

Clarissa lumbered out of the mistress's office, not caring how much noise she made as she went to get her book. Cora and Treffie came up beside her and sat down on the locker. Treffie's pale face was anxious. "I wanted a sister for my dolly," she whispered. She looked down at the book on her knee. "A book is no good to me."

"Now don't be putting on a long face," Cora told her. "Santa knew what you needed to bring out yer readin' voice."

"It's true, Treffie," said Clarissa. "Reading is a lot of fun. It will knock the loneliness out of your head for hours at a time. You'll love *Heidi*."

"I don't know how to read," Treffie said, her eyes downcast. "I don't remember ever pitching me eyes on books before I cum here. Sure, I don't know what the black marks mean."

"You'll learn here, then," Cora promised. "Fast, too, when yer feeling better and Miss Ellis gets ahold of you."

Treffie's eyes brightened. "I'll be glad then."

Clarissa sulked all the way through the salmon and rice dinner. She tried to listen to her sister-self talking. *You can't be getting two gifts when everyone else gets one. You like the book you got. It's yours; you don't have to take it back to the library.* It's just as well you can't have the muff. If you wore it on the sled, Peter and Jakot might grab it and that would be the last you'd see of your mother's gift.

After dinner Clarissa went into the study and sat at the table, leafing through an issue of *Among The Deep Sea Fishers*, a magazine founded by Dr. Grenfell to tell the world about the people of his mission. The "Children's Page" had a story about the need for a Home. Clarissa looked at the sketch of the brick orphanage. Little girls, in wide-brimmed hats, flowered dresses and striped and plain knitted stockings, were walking up the concrete steps under an arch above the entrance. Clarissa imagined The Home being just as perfect in real life. It likely could be, if everyone followed the motto: "A long pull, a strong pull and a pull together."

She searched until she found the Christmas issue from 1915. She read, as she had last year, about her first Christmas away from home. She was at the Grenfell Hospital. On Christmas Day, every patient well enough was moved to the same ward. There were shrieks of delight when Santa Claus stood in the doorway with a bag slung over his shoulder. Clarissa's eyes brightened as she read about herself: ". . . Clarissa Dicks found somebody's lap to bury her head in and tried valiantly to surpass George in screaming. It was impossible for Santa Claus to make any advance, whatever gift he offered the two, and not until he had removed his mask would Clarissa

deign to peek through her fingers and give him a shy smile as
she accepted a big darling doll."

Clarissa smiled at this image of herself. She closed the
magazine and pushed herself to her feet. She lifted her chin.
I'm not a baby and I am not going to cry. She'd take a lesson
from Johnny, a little boy from Labrador. Once, after some
older boy had picked on him, Clarissa had gone to comfort
him. He had shrugged, and said with a grin: "Whenever I feel
like crying, I smile instead. That's what everyone wants to see:
a bright face like a bright day."

She would lie in bed, snug under her blankets and counterpane and read her Christmas book. *Little Women* was sure
to make her smile.

11
MISSUS FRANCES'S
BOXING DAY VISIT

On Boxing Day, Clarissa and Cora stood on the orphanage steps looking towards a shed across from the orphanage. Missus Frances would soon be on her way to take gifts to children in isolated places. The girls watched a Labrador driver rigging his komatik with a rifle, axe, sleeping bag, medical kit, snowshoes, and whale meat and blubber for his team of seven husky dogs. An extra pair of sealskin mittens hung over the horns of his sled. Harbour dogs were barking excitedly as the driver got lashings and ropes out of the shed, and tackled his huskies. When he drew up by the orphanage door, the yelping dogs were so excited that if Missus Frances hadn't hurried out and got into the deerskin-lined seat, there was a chance they might have broken their traces. It was good that cold weather was holding. If it had gone mild and then frozen, the jagged ice path would have been like knives against the feet of the dogs as they ran.

Uncle Aubrey brought out gifts and supplies, and the driver piled them into the coach box fastened to the komatik with leather cords. Missus Frances wrapped herself in a sealskin robe and the Eskimo driver snapped his walrus-hide whip. "Ohoosh! Ooisht!" rose in the frosty air. The dogs made a rush over crisp snow shining like glass under an ice-blue sky.

Clarissa's mind followed the komatik over the hills, black branches shaking away snow as they flicked against its sides. The driver's voice would be sharp against the ears of the dogs. "Ouk!" turned the team right; "Urrah! Urrah!" turned it left, and "Ouk oo-ist, hoo-eet!" made the husky dogs go forward. She thought about the komatik going up over Fox Farm Hill, past Dr. Grenfell's castle, past the Tea House and the strange box wrapped in snow like an unopened Christmas box.

Only once had Clarissa gone past Tea House Hill and around the pond. "It is twelve miles to Devil's Pond, and it is the dead of winter, so dress warmly," had been Miss Elizabeth's caution last year. Clarissa had pulled on extra clothes, including her double mittens, and had hurried out to sit on the sled drawn by a team of husky dogs, their fur parting like pompoms in the wind. Cold wind had come like a naked blade against her face as the dogs jolted her over high ground and low, and down into the valley where the silver skim of Devil's Pond lay. The komatik came back down Fox Farm Hill and along the road. It pulled up by the orphanage, and the driver hauled out his walrus-hide whip and called "Aw" to stop the dogs. By then, frost was biting down on Clarissa's fingers so hard she could barely get her hands on her crutches. When she did, she started up the steps, leaning heavily on her crutches and crying. Tears had frozen on her eyelashes by the time she reached the top step. Miss Elizabeth held the door open without speaking as Clarissa dragged herself inside. She stood there trying to fold her fingers inside her palms to stop the burning pain. *I'm a crybaby,* she thought. *I won't ever get to go on a sled again.* And she hadn't.

Now Clarissa stared wistfully, visualizing Missus Frances and her driver going past deer standing silently, and snowbirds rustling in the trees. Like a ship in a headwind, the sled would ride over the hills and dip down into the rutted valleys on its way to settlements such as Flowers Cove. The mistress would be gone for two days. Anything could happen on such a trip. Clarissa hoped no harm would follow or meet Missus Frances. The brake stick could snap off the komatik going downhill . . . the dogs could get loose or tangled up in their traces . . . her driver could run off . . .

As soon as the mistress and the dog team were out of sight, Clarissa turned to Cora. "We should go see Esther. I'd like to take her a hard knob candy and a book."

Cora shrugged. "Miss Elizabeth would skin us if she found out. You know she has warned us not to go marming around the harbour – mixing up with the likes of the harbour crowd."

Clarissa looked at her. "It will always be like this," she said flatly, "one lot of people thinking they are finer than another lot, even though we are all from the same first skin."

"You mean Adam's skin?" Cora looked at her sceptically.

Clarissa rolled her eyes. "Well, I didn't mean Santa's skin."

* * *

Missus Frances, her face windburned, came back looking sad. She stood before the children at breakfast and told them that she and her driver had stopped at a small hut made of crude boards, just a hovel with a sod roof. They had found a mother with children scantily clad pressed against her, hiding their faces in the folds of her ragged dress. A baby lay in a wooden crate, diapered in moss and wrapped in sheep's wool. Their Christmas tree stood as bare as the trees outdoors, even plainer. The trees outdoors were decorated with snow and ice crystals. During the night the children's father, thinking he had heard the sad cry of a trapped rabbit, dressed and made for the woods, hoping to bring his family a Christmas dinner. The mother was waiting anxiously for him when Missus Frances and her driver showed up.

The mistress looked around the dining room at her charges; there was a quaver in her voice as she finished her story. "The children lost their dreary look at the sight of Christmas coming by dog team. They were timid at first. Each reached shyly to take an orange, looking at it in their hand as if they were seeing the sun come up for the first time. One little boy tried to eat it, peel and all. He shivered as the zest of the orange touched his tongue. Those children would be happy for warm stockings to put their feet in, never mind having them to hang up on Christmas Eve."

Clarissa wished she could give the children her porridge – wished, too, she could go home and let one of the children take her place.

12
NEWS OF CLARISSA'S FAMILY

New Year's Day came and went with the burning of the Clavie. The boys split up old blubber casks and set them alight, smoking the sky to open the new year.

Six days passed and then it was Old Christmas Day. It came with a golden shine on trees, their dark limbs lifted like fingers in crystal gloves. Conkerbells hung off the orphanage and fence like silver carrots with a golden shine. The older girls got busy taking down Christmas decorations that trimmed the dining room windows and walls. Clarissa helped undress the tree until it was as bare as when it left the forest near Fox Farm Hill.

"Bad luck it will be indeed if we keep any sign of Christmas after its twelve days are spent," Ilish tutted, shooing the older boys to the task of taking away the tree. They laughed and poked at one another, and pulled sprigs off the tree, tossing them into the faces of anyone near. Miss Elizabeth heard them and put a stop to their bantering with a flash of her eyes in their direction. Owen and Peter picked up the battered tree with mournful faces, as if they were lifting a dead body. They dragged it outdoors and through the snow to the shed where it would be limbed for firewood. Other boys went off to the woods to cut a turn of wood for the furnace and fireplaces. They were always watchful for the footin's of bears and foxes as they hauled the wood home by sled.

Clarissa stared out her dormitory window, feeling that the spirit of Christmas had closed its wings forever. She hadn't minded that December carried more night than day when she had Christmas to anticipate. Now that January was here, she hated to wake to night staining daylight, and not fading until after breakfast.

She brightened at the thought that she would have another special day to look forward to. It would carry her through this cold month, and the vexation of being dragged to school by boys who wanted to be running on their own. Her twelfth birthday was coming. She rolled her eyes at the sight of Peter turning heel over hand in the snow. It was bad luck that they had been born on the same day, if not in the same year. In a few days she would have to share a birthday with him. She and Peter would blow out the candles together, his head leaning in towards the cake as if it was all his.

She had been almost ten before she learned the real month and day of her birthday. She was about to celebrate her birthday with Jakot and Ettie in August when Nurse Smith came back from a trip away. She told Clarissa and Miss Elizabeth that she had dropped in on Mrs. Dicks in Humbermouth, and found out that Clarissa had turned nine on the twenty-seventh of January.

"Well, my child," she had announced, "your father is a train engineer, and your mother looks after a kitchen full of children."

"Boys or girls?" Clarissa had asked in awe, wanting to touch the nurse for having been in the same place as her family. There were so many questions racing after each other that they piled up, clogging her mind, even while the nurse was answering her first question.

"Likely a half-dozen of one and half a dozen of the other, I should think," the nurse said, smiling. "You will celebrate a real birthday now, with your true date, instead of getting lumped in with the other children who have birthdays in August."

"Yes, we'll wait for January," said Miss Elizabeth, ignoring Clarissa's disappointed look at being cheated out of her birthday for that year.

* * *

On the Saturday following Old Christmas Day, Jakot and Owen shovelled a path from the orphanage to the road; school began again on Monday. Clarissa stood on the steps watching them. Then she made her way down the icy steps to the ground where she looked longingly at boys and girls tossing snowballs at one other, laughing and slobbering into their mitts. She wanted to pelt all of them with snowballs. Instead, she sat making tunnels in the snow with her crutches, and building pyramids with her hands. Cora and Treffie joined her, digging big holes in the snowdrifts.

The boys soon finished their shovelling, and began to build a fort. They called to the girls to build their own fort, so they could have a battle. Clarissa sat on the ground, helping to dig the hole that would be the girls' fort. She could hear the boys yelling: "Ours 'll be bigger than yours." The boys were using the shovels they had been given to dig snow away from around the orphanage.

Clarissa swung herself inside the girls' fort.

"You can't be in the fort," Peter called. "We're going to war."

"I'll come," she said, lifting a resolute chin.

"You can't come. If there's anything wrong with your legs, you can't be conscripted."

"But it's just a toy war. We're using snowballs, not cannonballs."

"In with you then," he said, shrugging.

The girls squealed and shouted, firing snowball after snowball until Peter screamed in triumph, "We've made the most hits. You girls come out with your arms up."

"But my crutches will fall down," Clarissa called back.

"That's the fun," he said grinning. "Surrender with your face and eyes in a snowbank."

Clarissa pressed her armpits down on her crutches and tried to balance herself on the lumpy snow. She would meet the enemy eye to eye. *I'm not going to fall on my face,* she told herself, just before she slipped and went down.

Cora looked at Clarissa sympathetically. "We'll go indoors and play Snakes and Ladders."

"We could build a snow woman," said Treffie, coming up beside Clarissa.

"There's no such thing," said Cora, going up the steps.

"There will be," Treffie called, "when I'm finished."

Miss Elizabeth was just opening the door to come outside when the wind veered up like a demon, grabbing at her coat and swirling her shawl around her head. Her muskrat hat sailed into the air. The fierce wind pushed back the door and then slammed it in her face. "Newfoundland, this wild plantation," she muttered. "What an adventure this has turned out to be!"

The wind settled as suddenly as it had come. Cora and

Clarissa looked at each other and burst out laughing. "Too bad she didn't say a naughty word and have to wash out her own mouth," Cora said with a wicked grin.

13
A CLOSE CALL

"I dare you to walk across the ice on Bottom Brook, fraidy-cat," Imogene taunted Clarissa. "You've got crutches. That's the same as two gaffs."

"You can't walk; see if you can swim," Peter ragged her.

"Fraidy-cat, fraidy-cat!" The voices of Imogene and Peter yanked on her ears like hooks.

Cora's voice was anxious. "Don't go. They're playing a fool's game."

Clarissa ignored her, moving cautiously until she was standing on the frozen surface of the brook. She pulled back as a tinkling sound rose in the sharp air, the same noise she heard whenever she stepped on a shiny rind of ice over a puddle on the road. She tried to keep her balance as a grey line snaked through the freshwater ice. The ice broke and Clarissa toppled into black water. It widened around her and a piece of ice scraped her cheek and nose like the edge of a dull knife.

This is no way to go to Heaven, Clarissa thought wildly, *my birthday coming and all.* "Dr. Grenfell," she called foolishly. She didn't know why she called him. He wasn't there, and if he had been he would think she had done a terrible thing: risking the gift of life God had given her. Never mind that he had done it so many times, travelling on the ice with his komatik and dog team, even when he was warned that the ice wasn't safe. But he risked his life trying to save others. He hadn't done it on a silly dare.

Owen and Peter dragged Clarissa from the water. They and two other boys carried her barrow-style towards the orphanage. Shivers took over her body and her knees were icy knobs inside her cold braces. Her sodden woollen stockings and drawers dragged. *No wonder sheep run from rain; their wet wool must be a barrel of heaviness*, she thought ruefully.

Uncle Aubrey met the children at the door of the orphanage. He got Owen's explanation as he lifted Clarissa into his arms. He tut-tutted. "There you go – off on ice when you can't walk on land. What possessed you?"

Her teeth chattering, Clarissa answered, "The ice went smooth out over the brook from the land. I thought it was fastened, but then it cracked."

The caretaker's boots thumped down over the basement stairs. With Clarissa still in his arms, he went past the laundry room with its humongous tubs, its scrub boards and ironing boards, past racks and bins for sorting clothes, past a black pot-bellied, cast-iron stove laid with flatirons.

In a back room there was an enormous wood-burning iron stove. The waft from a dozen loaves of bread baking in the large oven filled Clarissa's nose. Cora's mother, a slight, worried-looking woman, was at the end of a long work table, kneading bread. A hairnet covered her dark hair, pulled straight back from her face into a fat roll. She shook her head at the sight of Clarissa, and ran to get a blanket that hung on a line by a little coal stove. Clarissa thought, *It's too bad she*

never has time to be a mother to Cora and Suzy and Owen.
Once when Cora had tried to talk to her mother, Clarissa
heard her answer tiredly, "Sure, you'll have to stop your chatter. You're moidering my brain." Clarissa imagined her
thoughts getting so mixed up her words wouldn't come out
right.

Myra, one of the helpers and a former orphanage inmate,
was at a metal sink washing dishes. "Dear me," she said.
"You'm a sight."

Soon Missus Frances was bearing down on her. "Clarissa,
you wretch, you've lost your crutches and broken your braces.
You'll have new crutches in a few days, but you will sit until
then. That will be punishment enough. You will likely sneeze
your way through your birthday this year and maybe find yourself over in the hospital with inflamed lungs."

In the hospital! In bed! Clarissa thought wildly. *Never
again!*

But as she lay in bed that night heat crept across her face
and lay on her cheeks like hot pokers. Her body felt peeled
. . . raw . . . tired. Someone washed her and then packed her
in softness. The edge of something cold was pressed to her
lips until they opened. A cool flow poured down her throat.
She floated above her pain, and then she was falling down
through time. The hands of a grandfather clock revolved
backwards; the pages of a calendar flipped back. Clarissa was
getting smaller and smaller, shrinking into the little girl she
used to be, a long time ago.

She surfaced through her delirium crying, "Nurse Smith!"
Her eyes opened to the walls of the orphanage infirmary. She
was wrapped in cold blankets and wearing an ice cap. An ice-
filled water bottle lay on her feet. Cora was wetting her lips as
Imogene looked on.

* * *

Clarissa had missed her birthday, but Missus Frances had saved her a mixture of Gibraltar sweets, peppermint knobs, butter rocks and a card of beads to ring into a bracelet. Her best birthday gift was from her mother. She would no longer have to hobble to the library to read *Alice's Adventures in Wonderland* over and over to keep her courage up.

She lay in bed sucking on a sweet and reading her book: a gift – if not a letter – from home.

14

QUARANTINED AND A SWEET LESSON

Clarissa's eyes opened in bewilderment. Daylight was coming through the window. She sat up thinking she had slept in and another morning would begin without breakfast. She looked around and saw that the other girls were still asleep. They had all slept in. There was the sound of footsteps in the hall, and then a knock came on the door. "Up, Girls! Just because there's no school is no reason to lie abed all day," Ilish called.

No school! Clarissa smiled to herself. She stayed very quiet, stretching her legs as much as she could, despite the aching in her limbs. She could spend time reading after she had finished her mending, darning and dusting chores.

The other children awoke as if pulled from sleep into a wonderful daydream. "No school?" Celetta asked, her heavy eyelids opening only a slit.

"Nooo schooool." Imogene dragged on the words, clearly disappointed. An arithmetic test had been slated for today, and she always got a hundred percent.

"Dusting and polishing, that's what we'll be doing," moaned Becky.

At breakfast Missus Frances explained, "The orphanage has been quarantined for six weeks because influenza is in the harbour. We don't want thirty little mortals dying of flu."

"'Tis a blind lookout, that's what it is. So many children in St. Anthony wandering around with their lips at each other's tin cups," Cora's mother said later. She poked a strand of Cora's hair behind her ear. "Sure, we're to guard this place with diligence. Thank God, 'tis not Spanish influenza: the sickness that took so many poor mortals a few years back."

Clarissa nodded at Cora's mother and then moved as fast as she could to get to the study room, before she was waylaid to do chores. She stayed there reading all morning, expecting to be hauled off at any moment to mend or dust. It wasn't until after lunch that Ilish called her into the mistresses' lounge. She laid a cloth and a bottle of lemon wash on a chair. "Dust-and-shine time," she said with a flicker of a smile as she went out the door. Clarissa leaned on one crutch and, with her good hand, dusted a wooden table, leaving a fresh, tangy smell in the air. Her mouth felt dry, and the dish of candy the mistresses kept in their quarters drew her, tantalized her. Usually she resisted. This time she reached out her hand to take one sweet. Her crutch slipped and she almost fell to the floor. She got a firmer grip, and her hand tightened over a striped hard knob. She lifted the big candy to her mouth and closed her lips around it. Her eyes shut with the pleasure of having a sweet to suck when it wasn't a special occasion.

Suddenly she heard a stir in the room. She opened her eyes quickly. Miss Elizabeth was standing directly in front of her. Clarissa tried to swallow the knob, but it caught in her throat. She coughed and the candy fell to the floor in front of the mistress. Miss Elizabeth stood eyeing her silently, her eyes like bullets. Clarissa hated the silence almost as much as the words that followed it. "Clarissa," the mistress said in a contemptuous voice, "you have broken one of the Ten Commandments again."

She said "again" as if there was no hope for her charge. Once before, Clarissa had pocketed some candy for herself and Cora. Imogene, whose head, Clarissa decided, was filled with nothing but gossip, had seen them sucking on the sweets. She had snitched to Miss Elizabeth that Clarissa had bucked candy.

Missus Frances had admonished the children not to be carrying tales, but when the busy noshers did, Miss Elizabeth rewarded them with approving smiles and sweets.

"You will eat your meals in the lobby for a week," Miss Elizabeth said sternly, her hands on her hips. Her arms, with their dry, pointed elbows, stuck out like handles on a jug.

Clarissa looked at her. Then she went back to her dusting. She wanted to smile for getting such a blessed punishment. The lobby wasn't so bad, especially for breakfast. She could flush her hated porridge down the toilet. It was better than getting her mouth washed out with a hunk of lye soap. She shuddered, remembering that taste.

Although Miss Elizabeth left the candy dish where it was, Clarissa knew that the temptation to take sweets again would be bridled by a sour memory. *Anyway, nothing tastes good after you've eaten it,* she thought with a shrug that almost knocked her off her crutches.

Clarissa passed the playroom on her way back from dusting. She had no mind to be with the girls from her dormitory, sitting around playing Snakes and Ladders – squealing when they got the highest number of pips. It was one of the few games she enjoyed. But not today. She would go to her room and read.

Ilish brought Clarissa's supper to the dormitory bath and toilet room with an apologetic look on her young, round face. She laid the tray across the sink. Then she got Clarissa a chair. After Ilish left, Clarissa started to eat the vegetable stew. She stopped, her fork in midair, and picked up the glass of water with her left hand. She took a big gulp, and then another; here by herself she could drink the water whenever – and however she wanted to. She drained the glass and then she ate the rest of the stew, brown bread and tapioca pudding. Looking at herself in the mirror, she muttered, with her finger moving in the air as if she were writing lines, "You must not steal candy. You must not steal. You must not . . . You must . . . You . . . !" She licked out her tongue, pretending it was at Old Keziah. Then she washed and left the lobby.

Clarissa changed into her nightclothes and went to bed, pulling the sheets up to her chin. *This place,* she thought, grimacing, *is full of snakes and ladders: snakes like mistresses, and ladders a girl can't climb to get away from tattlers.*

15

SURPRISE FROM THE SKY

The quarantine ended and the pupils went racing back to school, all except those who were slated to pull Clarissa. Jakot and Peter took turns yanking the sled over the thinning snow. Once the roads were bare, Clarissa would be able to drag herself along on her crutches. It was better than having to be beholden to the orphanage boys.

The boys stopped the sled beside the school and Clarissa picked up the crutches Peter had thrown on the ground. She hauled herself up on them, and ambled up the steps into the school. A stillness settled inside her as she sat in her seat. When Miss Ellis spoke, her voice sounded as if it was far away and muffled. Clarissa's head dropped and slid along her arm. She awoke as if from a blow. Her fingers were caught between the edge of the desk and the school ma'am's ruler.

"This is no place to sleep." Miss Ellis's voice was stern. "Especially not today." Her eyes darted to the window, then back. She smiled and her tone turned pleasant. "We have a very big surprise."

The children lifted their heads, holding themselves quiet as if they were afraid to move for fear of missing the announcement. Their ears perked to a distant, unfamiliar sound getting louder by the second. All of a sudden, a roar filled the air. The startled school ma'am ran to the window followed by her pupils. Clarissa could not believe what she was seeing: a giant, grey craft, shaped like a huge bird, hovered above the iced-in harbour. The other children dashed out of the school, leaving the door wide open. Clarissa followed them. Miss Ellis came out behind her and closed the door. Then she, too, rushed past Clarissa, who tried to hurry for fear the strange craft would disappear into the sky before she got to it. The younger children from the lower classroom had been running as fast as their legs could carry them. Now they hung back as the big bird landed and skidded to a halt.

"An aeroplane," Miss Ellis explained, her eyes shining. "That's what you are seeing. The first plane that has ever landed in St. Anthony. Be patient until the pilot cuts his engine."

The pupils, and people who had gathered from around the harbour, stood motionless, staring, waiting for the man in charge of flying the metal bird to appear.

The pilot pulled back the door and stepped out of the plane. He was dressed in a leather jacket breasted with medals, his britches tucked into shiny leather boots. He ran towards the crowd, his cheeks curving into brackets around a wide smile as he announced, "Major Fisson from St. John's at your service."

Major Fisson was not just a pilot. He was also a mailman. Amid the commotion of people gathering to see the plane, he passed out parcels to carriers from the hospital and the orphanage. Miss Ellis and Miss Janes, the younger pupils' school ma'am, didn't seem surprised when they received a package each.

Miss Ellis turned from speaking to Major Fisson. "Back to

school now," she ordered the children. She added, "The pilot was generous enough to bring a packet of silent pictures for Dr. Grenfell's Magic Lantern. Perhaps they will star Charlie Chaplin, the silent screen star you love so much. You will see the pictures later. For now, you can write an essay on the first time you saw an aeroplane."

Clarissa's mind was brimming with the thought that some-day she could be a passenger on the air ship. The pilot would fly her up into the sky, away from the earth, away from the orphanage. He would fly her home. She followed the other children reluctantly. They were all dragging their feet and look-ing back at the airman, who seemed to be as much of a star as Charlie Chaplin.

"I'm going to be a flyer," Peter called to Jakot. "I'm going to fly over to Canada."

"Hush, you braggart!" Jakot called back.

Clarissa smiled. She knew that after today, all the boys and maybe some of the girls would dream of being a flyer.

While the other children wrote about the air ship, Clarissa decided to write something else, something that was pressing so hard on her mind she couldn't ignore it.

"Up, Clarissa," Miss Ellis called, gesturing with her hand, as soon as she saw that Clarissa was finished writing. "Read us your essay."

Clarissa stood up, nipping her scribbler against her crutch as she went up to the school ma'am's desk. She sat down on the big chair and opened the scribbler. She remembered Miss Ellis's instructions: Lean forward while you are speaking so that listeners see you as being in charge. Clarissa relaxed and tipped forward like she did when she was on crutches. Her voice rose and settled against the ears of the pupils, whose eyes widened in surprise.

"Some of you," Clarissa began, "have resented having to pull me on a sled to school. You would rather be on the sled with someone pulling you. But none of you would want to be on my crutches, or have my feet. I have wanted to put on shoes like other girls wear: shiny shoes with little black buttons. My legs are in heavy braces, my body trapped, while yours run free. You dream of flying; I dream of walking.

"Imagine what it would be like to take a turn on my crutches, walking upstairs, downstairs, up hills and down hills. Imagine wanting to be able to run and play games. Imagine the feeling of not being able to do that everyday forever. No, not forever," Clarissa added, shaking her head. "If it were forever, I would not be able to bear it."

Peter cupped his chin in his hands as if his head was filling with the weight of her words. Miss Ellis tapped his fingers with her ruler, and he dropped his hands to his desk. He looked past Clarissa as if he was listening to something else, but he couldn't escape what was going into his ears. None of them could, and it was not only the words. It was the sound of Clarissa's voice, strong and full. It was not handicapped. Cora let out a sob as Clarissa finished: "I am crippled, but I am not a cripple."

That afternoon when the boys pulled Clarissa home on the sled, the only sharp sounds she heard were those coming from the runners going over rocks sticking up through the snow. She was glad, even though she knew her words would soon be forgotten by bullies who felt good only when they were making other children sad.

16
A SPRING VISIT

Except for a necklace of slob rinding the shore, the ice had melted, leaving the harbour looking dark and cold. Then one morning in late March, Clarissa looked through the window and saw, just out from the beach below the orphanage, large pans of ice bobbing in the harbour. They held a lot of dark spots. "The seals are whelping," she yelled to the other girls. They scattered from their beds and ran together to the window, almost knocking Clarissa off her crutches.

"Babies. Well, if that wouldn't square your eyeballs. The seals are pupping." Quiet Becky breathed her words in awe. Tiny, fluffy white balls were sliding from the dark bodies of mother seals.

Through the open window, the girls watched saddleback seals and adult harps trimming ice pans, paddling and walloping. Then there was a rush of dark figures towards the floes. Local fishermen were out to catch the snail-like creatures squirming across the pans. Some of the seals were shot, their blood staining the ice. Others slipped off the pans, escaping into the water. Soon there wouldn't be a seal in sight. In homes all along the harbour, women waited, some of them desperate for the rich meat to feed their families; there were children near starvation. Clarissa watched a baby seal lift its head as if to mewl; its whiskers were like stiff, black threads. She cringed and turned away as Jakot clubbed it. The dead seal would be brought to the orphanage to be added to the vegetable stew. Clarissa hated to see newborn seals killed. She wished the sealers could wait until the seals were three weeks old. Then they would be as dark and their bite as vicious as the bites of older seals. She tightened her lips, resigned. To sealers and mothers in the harbour, the cries of children with empty bellies were stronger than the mewling of white-coats.

Clarissa followed the other children down to the beach, hoping to see seals haul themselves up on the ice. The sea panted under pans scrunching against each other. Dovekies perched on outer pans lying in the ocean like little, white islands. The birds lifted into the sky and lay motionless as if dozing on the wind. By the time Clarissa reached the beach, all the seals had disappeared, some into the sea, others into the sealers' sculp pans.

Shouts came from harbour children clambering on the ice. They jumped from one blue-hemmed clump to another, as if daring the sea to topple them. There were squeals as cakes of ice wobbled. An ice pan tipped and Rory, a harbour boy, slid into the cold water. The other boys pulled him out shivering and blabbering. The boys were copying pans in sight of mothers shaking their heads at the boys' mischief.

Clarissa watched a water duck battering between ice pans. She was startled by the crack of a shotgun. The bird was soon hanging limp in the hunter's hand. She turned away from the sight, only to see harbour boys stoning bull birds that the wind had blown out on the ice. *Idle and cruel*, she thought, before realizing the birds were likely for a sweet pot of soup the boys' families rarely enjoyed.

The ice groaned and creaked; by afternoon, glinting pans of ice had raftered. From a distance, they looked like tiny bergs. During the night, the ice left as quickly as it had come, carried away by tides moving in and out the harbour.

In the morning when Clarissa looked through the window she let out a sigh of relief. There was no sign of seals and ice pans, and no show of blood to mark the fishermen's rites of spring.

17

SPRING AWAKENING

Spring came stirring through the ground, breaking out in a laugh through the stream by the orphanage. Dead leaves danced in the wind, then scuttled along the ground.

The first half of April brought dark clouds bruising the sky above an ocean of white-tailed waves. There were days when white lines of rain cut the sky, and wind blowing in from the ocean popped bubbles on the harbour water.

Uncle Aubrey stood in the arch of the orphanage door, shaking his head and muttering, "The likes of this wind is makin' ose eggs clutch stones to steady themselves."

"April, I hate April!" Clarissa moaned as she ran her finger through a dull film on the dormitory window. Rain fell as if the sky itself had broken and was cascading down to drown everyone on earth. At this time of the year, dubbed the cow days of April, it was best for Clarissa to stay inside the orphanage. It would be hard for her to crutch her way through those last patches of snow now lying like blankets dragged through mud.

Easter Monday brought relief, not from the weather, but from a Christian custom at the orphanage. The children had to be quiet and solemn during the days before Easter in memory of Christ's suffering. Now they were free to laugh and play, as if the days of a funeral wake had ended. They would celebrate Christ's resurrection with coloured eggs.

Clarissa pushed her crutches as fast as she could down the stairs to the dining room. On each enamel plate were eggs dyed green, mauve and blue, and a thick slice of white bread. Not a crumb of black bread in sight!

After supper, Missus Frances called Clarissa into her office. "An Easter parcel came with your Christmas gift from home, Clarissa. It contained jelly beans. I'll keep the candy in my desk and you can come for some now and then. Be kind and don't tell the other children about your good fortune."

Clarissa nodded, even though she wanted the candy in her hand and in her pocket – a gift from her mother to her. Missus Frances should have no say in the matter.

"Here you are then." The mistress smiled, showing her gold tooth, as she dropped a handful of jelly beans into Clarissa's gimp pocket.

Clarissa thanked the mistress. Then she clumped her way to the dormitory and sat on her bed. She dropped a jelly bean into her mouth, and bit into it, surprised at how it clung to her teeth instead of making a harsh crack like hard candy.

* * *

A cold night had brought a damp morning with vapour rising above the sea. The children shivered outside the orphanage. Some of them were growing too big for their winter clothes and their Beanie boots had gotten worn and wet from a winter randying in the snow. Young children were jumping up and down the steps to keep the dampness out of their bones. Mrs.

Budden, the new housemother, wouldn't let the children inside the porch to warm up, and she showed no intentions of letting them randy in the playroom. She wanted them to run about and make their own heat.

Fannie Appleby, who worked in the kitchen, motioned to the children to come into the basement. The older boys were in there stacking wood.

Clarissa looked at Fannie to thank her just as Miss Elizabeth hurried to jaw the kitchen worker for being so lenient. "This must be what Dr. Grenfell calls 'the fun of mothering an orphanage,'" she grumbled.

Fannie tossed her bonneted head and exclaimed, "Hamburg and Beanie boots, with their sealskin leggings, can oblige a foot in every way if the weather is dry, but when 'tis drenching, they're a body's torment."

The mistress didn't answer. Instead, she turned and rushed back up the stairs, as if her body, in its long, dark dress under an ankle-length, white shawl, was being swept by a gale of wind.

Fannie's long, curly lashes swept upward in disdain. She laid a dry, crusted hand against her cheek and spoke with gumption. "Sure, the mistress came to a place where she figured the savages would lick her boots while freezing in theirs."

Clarissa was surprised at her words. Sometimes she felt that all the adults were against the children. She looked into Fannie's plain face and smiled.

* * *

In late April, the yellow bonnets of daffodils nodded above the earth. Morning glories followed near trees whose knobby knuckles would soon burst into fingers of green leaves. In no time, the land laid out a daisy chain of buttercups. Flocks of birds hopped over the green rug of spring; dandelions danced in the soft air. Sparrows tisped and chickadees went chick-a-dee-dee-dee in the newly sprung leaves.

Clarissa leaned on the veranda rail and tossed a piece of hard bread from her gimp pocket. As she listened to the rolling echo of a robin's song, a line from her *Royal Reader* hopscotched into her mind: *"Popping o'er the carpet, picking up the crumbs . . ."* A robin dropped to the ground and looked around, hopping and dipping; it poked a hole in the soil and ferked up a worm. Then the robin flew away with its supper in its beak. Soon the robin would be sitting on a nest full of bright blue eggs holding the promise of baby robins. Clarissa thought of the eggs tucked away inside her body. She hoped all of them wouldn't crack and drop out of her before she could start a baby.

She hadn't seen the Christmas baby since he had been under the tree. He was likely adopted now and shortened. She had heard the young helpers chattering among themselves that Baby Nunatik wasn't going home to his native family because the doctors at the hospital didn't agree with his parents' way of treating his sickness. The father had scratched the baby's body with needles and cut his scalp to the bone with a knife, letting the blood spurt; then his mother poured salt into the wound to clean his blood. The parents believed the baby's screams would help stretch his lungs.

* * *

Clarissa heard sounds of banging as she pushed open the basement door. She followed the sounds to the cobbler's shop. The older boys were busy fitting a shoe at a time over an iron last. Using a sharp knife from the cobbling box on the floor, they took a piece of tap from a larger, worn-out shoe, and sized it to fit the sole of a smaller one. Then they hammered it on with brass tacks. The patched and remade shoes would have to do the children until the *Prospero* squeezed its way through ice far out in the bay and sailed into the harbour. The children waited all spring for shoes to arrive from Canada and the United States, hoping to get a pair not patched. All of them except Clarissa. She got extra taps on a pair of gaiters, or a change of gaiters if she had outgrown her old ones.

Clarissa eyed the children from the doorway of the play-room. She swallowed in longing as they discarded their winter skin boots and were fitted with brown or black shoes. Treffie's eyes brightened at the sight of her pair. She stared at her name printed on a piece of paper which would be placed in her shoes when they were in the locker she shared with two other girls. Clarissa thought about the time she had been given a pair of shoes. Someone else had worn them out, scuffing along roads, over hills, hippity-hopping through summer.

Clarissa watched Treffie, in her new shoes, join the girls in the schoolyard for a game of hopscotch. The little girl helped draw hopscotch blocks. Afterwards, she got to toss the penny into the air. It fell closest to Cora. She began the game, hopping on one leg, while kicking a flat rock. She kicked the rock from the parlour pudge square through the centre block, called the boiler, and through the next set of blocks to the parlour pudge at the end, and back again without getting her rock on the line. Treffie was so concerned about scuffing her new shoes, she went out on her first try.

Whenever Clarissa sat watching the other children running, skipping and playing hopscotch, she felt as if she were behind a glass wall. She wanted her own laughs and shouts to

shatter the wall and mingle with the voices of the other children. But she sat silently, wishing, hoping – *knowing* that one
day she would walk and run like everyone else.

Clarissa made her way to the sundeck out from the first
floor of the orphanage. From there she often watched full-
sailed schooners plowing through the heavy Atlantic seas to
the shelter of the harbour. Today she caught a glimpse of the
year's first icebergs. It was as if a winter wind had carved them
with a wild hand, and set the magnificent sculptures adrift. Far
out in the bay, they towered above the sea, translucent blue
lights arcing off them.

Clarissa imagined herself a mermaid, sitting with her mer-
man on a crystal ledge of their iceberg castle as it sailed dia-
mond-flecked waters. She stayed on the sundeck until the
world took a deep breath and held it in, and the sun slid like
a gold coin into the sea.

18

THE SCHOOL INSPECTOR

"Tomorrow," Miss Ellis announced, "Mr. Spence Hayward, the school inspector, is coming. He would visit every year if he could, but circumstances sometimes get in his way. When he knocks and I open the door, you shall stand and give this greeting: 'Good morning, Sir.'"

Peter's hand shot up, his fingers spread wide. "Miss, do we have to salute?" he asked boldly.

The school ma'am pursed her lips. "You do not."

"Bow?"

"No. Inspector Hayward is not King George of England."

Jude, a harbour boy, nicknamed Lumpy because he had a big lump of a head on a short neck, asked in a timid voice, "King Cole then?"

"I declare," said Miss Ellis, with an impatient jerk of her head that almost sent her brimmed hat flying, "some of you will go down in history in one certain way. Just do as I tell you, then sit in your seats with your backs straight, your hands on the desk and your feet flat on the floor. And mind the inspector. He has long hands and a stick to lengthen them."

Cora raised her hand, and when Miss Ellis nodded, "Yes,

Cora, what is your question?" she asked, almost in a whisper, her face reddening, "Miss, what's a school inspector?"

"You will find out soon enough," the school ma'am replied in a crisp voice. "I caution you all to tidy yourself before you come to school tomorrow. Make sure your finger-nails are clean and your hair combed. Try to appear civilized, and interested in what the inspector says."

Once the pupils were dismissed, most of them scattered outside. Some of them hung around to talk about the school inspector. Clarissa overheard an older pupil complain that he had been put in the corner once by a school inspector for not addressing him correctly. After the inspector left, the school ma'am put him in the corner again. "You made me appear unfit for my position," she said.

Clarissa was almost afraid to sleep that night for fear the inspector would ask her a question she didn't know. She didn't want to have the dunce cap placed on her head, and be put in the corner in front of a school inspector. She finally slipped into sleep and awoke long before the sound of the morning bell clanged through the dormitory.

* * *

At school, the pupils who had never seen an inspector sat fidg-eting in their seats and biting their lips.

Miss Ellis raised a dark eyebrow and said pointedly, "It is not just you who are being tested. I am also being judged on how well I manage a collection of orphans, heathens and poor ragamuffins."

The children looked at Miss Ellis and then at each other, as if they were trying to put each other in the right breed.

When the dreaded knock came, all eyes turned towards

the door, including Rory's. He was known for crossing his eyes and turning his upper eyelids inside out when Miss Ellis wasn't looking. Today he spat quickly on his fingers and ran them through his hair, trying to batten down his red curls.

"Face the front of the schoolroom," the school ma'am hissed as she hurried down the aisle to open the door and let in a little man whose stomach was so big he looked like an egg on legs.

Inspector Hayward's presence filled the room. It pressed in on Clarissa, frightening her. The other children jumped up from their seats, stood at attention and said: "Good morning, Sir," before Clarissa could get to her feet. The inspector's eyes flickered over her.

"Hang the inspector's coat in the cloakroom, Rory," said Miss Ellis in a level voice.

Rory made jerky movements as he rushed to take the stranger's coat and scarf. He looked dumbfounded as he disappeared into the cloakroom. He hurried out and back into a standing position beside his desk.

Looking at the children standing at attention, Miss Ellis reached out her hands, her fingers dipping as if to press the children back down into their places. They dropped like stones.

The inspector stood in front of the pupils, his stomach stretching his suspenders to the limit. "I assume you all know your times tables." His voice was stern.

A hand shot up. "I do, Sir. Me farder wants me to learn me sums so no merchant can cheat me." That was Simon, who often had to listen to chants of "Simon says" as he went up the road after school.

"I'm sure it would not make a sum of difference if he did," the inspector drawled. "You won't need to know how

many zeros are in a nonillion, since you will likely go no farther than a fisherman's boat and a poor man's lot."

"A nonillion has 30 zeros – in Britain, 54 zeros, Sir,"
Simon answered quickly.

"I suppose," the inspector said, "you all know what a cat-
o'-nine-tails is."

"I do, Sir," Peter said promptly. His hand shot up. He sat
waiting, with an imprudent look, until the inspector nodded
for him to go ahead. "It's a cat with nine tails, Sir, something
no one has ever seen here."

"I'll thank you not to be so saucy," was the inspector's
gruff reply.

Rory's fist reached into the air. Before the inspector could
give him a nod, Jakot said, "No cat could live in this harbour
with nine tails, Sir. Peter and his like would bob them.
Sometimes cats lose the one tail they have. Around here cats
don't even have nine lives. What with all the dogs."

"'Tis bad English, idn't it, Sir, to say cat o' nine tails?"
Rory offered.

The inspector's face turned as red as a rose fish. "Where
is your grammar?"

"She's dead, Sir."

"Are you making fun, using a joke here?" the inspector
asked, his face puffing up like a doughboy.

"No Sir, I can't make fun. I tries to 'ave it when I can, but
wit' all der work ter do in dis 'arbour, 'tis 'ard to 'ave it."

"Pronounce your *h*'s," the inspector said sternly. "It is
obvious that you have not been going to school long enough to
have *h* tacked on where it belongs in your speech. Up with you
in the corner to think about the word *elisions*."

"Yes, Sir. I don't mind, Sir." The boy jumped up.

"Did you know," the inspector asked with a glance in the

direction of Rory's back, "that in the Middle Ages, the fat of a dead redhead was used in poison?" He looked around the class-room with a dark countenance. When no one answered him, he lifted his voice and his toes at the same time. "You came from lowly Irish and English fishermen who crossed the sea because they were starving in their own countries. They didn't care about expanding their language or their minds. You must learn to mind your manners after coming from uncouth ancestors."

Clarissa knew that the orphan children tried to use "the King's English" in front of the mistresses. Inside the orphan-age, they called to each other, "Where are you going?" Outside the orphanage, she often heard them ask, in relaxed voices, "Where's yers off to?"

There were times when Clarissa wished she knew the beautiful French language in which some of her forebears had expressed themselves. The English nurses had taught her to speak "good" English. They disdained what they deemed to be Newfoundland's corruption of Irish and English speech. Some English workers and visitors sounded as if their tongues were fastened to the roofs of their mouths. If the orphans didn't understand them immediately, they got annoyed.

The English and Americans think they are better than us, Clarissa thought angrily. On impulse, she said, "I read that there were no forks in England until 1620. Commoners ate with their fingers, but so did kings and queens – and they went easy on bathing, too."

Inspector Hayward looked at her as if he was wondering where she was coming from. Then he shrugged and turned back to the class, his right elbow in his left hand, his right thumb under his chin. "I shall teach you how to say *three* instead of *tree* when you are counting. Your teacher can help correct some of your elisions later. Everyone with me now."

Clarissa looked at the pink under-thread of his tongue as he pressed it up behind his front teeth. It looked so funny she had all she could do to keep her face from splitting and letting out a laugh. She glanced at Cora, who was obviously fighting the same impulse. Just then Cora's lips burst open and a low, quick laugh slipped out. The inspector walked to her desk. He hit the ink bottle which sat in a round slot at the corner of the desk. The ink flew into the air and splashed down on the wooden floor, spreading like a shadow. He grabbed Cora by her collar and said, "I have a mind to stand you by the hot stove."

Clarissa was tempted to say, "She won't be able to say three then." Instead, she watched Cora pull away from his strong, hairy hand, coughing so hard that the inspector moved away from her.

"That boy in the corner is a noetic child, despite his disregard for standard English," the inspector said. The children all looked at him as if he had a foreign tongue in his mouth. He shouted, "Noetic means having intellect. It is not a difficult word and it is in the dictionary. If you learn words like it, people will think you are noetic – even if you are not." One frosty eyebrow lifted as if it were the bristling tail of a husky dog.

After admonishing Miss Ellis to uphold the English language with vigour and discipline, the inspector turned to the pupils. "That will be all for this visit," he said solemnly. He dipped his head in the direction of the school ma'am. Then he turned quickly and started to walk towards the door. The children stood up, all of them except Clarissa. She remained seated, thinking: *In future I shall stand only for a king – or a soldier back from war.*

Rory, his hair sticking up from his head like a curly mop,

turned from the corner with his eyelids inside out. Jakot pulled out his brown handkerchief and blew his nose, sounding like a foghorn. The inspector turned and looked at Jakot disapprovingly. "Be careful of where you make an emunctory."

Jakot looked like he was straining to go to the toilet as he spat out the strange word the inspector had thrown at him. "E'monkey," he said.

"Whisht!" Miss Ellis cautioned, putting a finger to the side of her mouth as if she didn't want the inspector's stay to be prolonged. The children stayed standing until the inspector had pulled on his coat and scarf and the door had closed behind him.

So that's what an inspector is, Clarissa thought, *someone whose stomach is so big it looks as if he swallowed a dictionary.* She hoped that circumstances would get in the way of him coming again.

19
THE GOVERNOR AND
HIS LADY

Treffie's pale face bent in wonder over a primrose peeping out of the ground. The bracelet of buttons on her wrist clattered as she picked the pink flower and lifted it to her nose before pushing it into a buttonhole. Spying an airy dandelion, she ran to it and bent down to blow the globe of knitted stars apart. She watched as they danced upon the wind.

Clarissa watched Treffie from the orphanage steps, hoping she would get well once summer came. Then she turned her attention to Peter and Jakot, who were digging a hole to plant a maypole. They had carefully removed all the branches of a tree, except for the plume at the top. Hipper, a new orphan whose real name was Harold, and Owen were making an archway of branches and coloured bows above the orphanage gates. Cora and Imogene were waiting to decorate the maypole with ribbons and paper for good luck.

Everyone was excited about being part of the special occasion. Clarissa thought about Missus Frances's announcement at breakfast that Sir William Allardyce, Governor of Newfoundland, was arriving from St. John's tomorrow. There would be a reception for him at The Home. She hoped he wasn't as full of big words as the inspector.

The next morning, Clarissa was about to get dressed when a knock came on the door. Missus Frances hurried in, smiling. "You are to dress for Sir William Allardyce today, Clarissa."

"Me?" Clarissa's mouth dropped open.

"Yes. You are going to meet Governor William Lamond Allardyce and Lady Elsie Elizabeth Allardyce, who are, even as we speak, tidying up at St. Anthony Inn after their voyage on *The Wisaria*. You can pass in any company, and so you are the child chosen to present a gift."

Clarissa looked at her, hesitating.

"Come on, Child. Don't falter. The Governor is a man the same as other men when he's not in uniform and wearing badges."

Clarissa was proud to be a Girl Guide in the Campfire Girl's Club, even if she couldn't do a lot of the things the other Guides did. Missus Frances helped her dress in her Girl Guide uniform: a long-sleeved navy dress with a red tie holding a gold maple leaf pin. She fastened Clarissa's belt with its shamrock buckle, and then laid a navy hat on her bouncy curls, slipping its leather strap under her chin.

"You're looking tidy enough," the mistress said, giving Clarissa the eye of approval as they hurried down the stairs and out the door. Clarissa stopped on the steps to smile up at Eddie Goodale, the Scout Master. He had often carried her around when she was small. He nodded encouragement as she made her way down the steps.

The orphanage children were used to seeing a scruffy, old, grey horse pulling a coal cart to the orphanage. They were not prepared for the big, black horse trotting through the gates. A crowd had gathered to watch this majestic animal pull a black carriage that had huge, spoked wheels. In the carriage sat Governor Allardyce and Lady Allardyce. Horse and carriage passed under the arch of branches and bows and a black-lettered WELCOME banner surrounded by flags. The driver occasionally halted the horse and carriage for people to snap the couple.

The orphanage children were ushered inside the orphanage to wait for their guests. Soon they were listening to Governor Allardyce as he stood on a locker and spoke about a paper mill opening up in Corner Brook, not far from the railway station. Clarissa felt a lonely stir. Her home was in Humbermouth, Corner Brook. There came a sudden surge of memory, bringing the clacking sound of a train going down a track. It was gone before she could hold it close.

Maybe, she thought, *there will be a railway station in St. Anthony someday, and a train track running down to Corner Brook. Then my father can drive the train right up to the orphanage, and take me home.* Dr. Grenfell would be happy not to have to take his dog team on the treacherous coastal journey of more than a hundred miles to Deer Lake Station so he could catch the train to Corner Brook. He often travelled to the United States by way of Corner Brook. The people there loved to hear about the poor white and dark natives of Newfoundland and Labrador.

Finally, at the prompting of Missus Frances, who was sitting behind her, Clarissa made her way to where Sir William Allardyce stood. He was dressed in a uniform trimmed with brass buttons and shining medals. Lady Allardyce stood there as sunny as a daffodil in the prettiest dress Clarissa had ever seen. She wore a wide-brimmed hat in the same shade of yellow. She smiled at Clarissa, who was trying to steady herself on her crutches so she could free her hand that held the gift the mistress had put into it. She bowed slightly, and passed the gift to Sir William Allardyce, wondering what was in it. It was likely a carving from the window display at the mission gift shop: a polar bear or a seal carved from a walrus tusk.

The next day Clarissa hopped along beside Miss Elizabeth as they went down the path to the wharf to wave goodbye to the Governor and Lady Allardyce. *If only my mother could see me now!* she thought wistfully.

That night she went to bed, not caring about the whispers of the other girls or the sound of "Pet!"digging into her ear.

20
SUMMER

It was June, and days fell out of nights well before breakfast, opening to the brightness and the scent of new flowers and leaves. Friday came, and with it the promise of no school for two days. Clarissa lifted her face to a wind that breathed softly against her skin. She marvelled at the smooth, milky-brown roads over which her crutches moved, leaving tiny imprints in the clay. Cora had gone ahead and was taking turns skipping rope and counting rounds with Becky on a grassy nob beside the road. She threw the rope over her shoulder and came back to where Clarissa had stopped to look down in a pothole full of water. Cora leaned over the water, and Clarissa giggled at the sight of her friend's image floating on an upside-down sky.

Simon, a fisherman's son whose eyes always looked hungry, and Peter passed the two girls. The boys were arguing loudly. Nicholas, the merchant's son, caught up with them. He taunted Peter. "You haven't got a father. You're nothing but a ragamuffin Dr. Grenfell took into the orphanage."

"Mind now, you don't know everything," Peter answered,

with a determined look in his green eyes. "I'm a good hand at adding and subtracting without rinding people. I'm looking to be an aeroplane flyer or a doctor."

"A fish doctor is what you'll be – and Simon too," Nicholas said with a sneer. Then he ran off down to the harbour wharf. Simon, indignant at being compared to a fish doctor: an orange beetle that clings to sick fish, yelled at Nicholas's back, "If me father never got his summer's haul, your father in his fancy hip-roofed house wouldn't give him a bag of flour for a nod towards next year, even though his fish helps keep your father in business."

The girls turned away from the boys and looked towards the harbour and the sea, now patterned like a mackerel's skin. Along the beach, small fishing boats that had lain bottoms up on the launch all winter, were being scraped and painted. Killicks were being made ready to anchor the boats in the harbour. Smoke no longer rose from funnels in store lofts, where the fishermen had spent cold months mending nets. Now the men were barking their nets in big-bellied pots. Other people were painting sheds and houses with tar and ochre. The strong, rich smell of oakum filled the air.

The girls passed a ramshackle house. In the back of it, a red rooster strutted around the inside of a small pen. Butterflies floated among white daisies growing by a grey shed that leaned beside a weather-blackened stage. The stage's legs had skewed under the weight of many summers. Now the high tide slapped and sucked its legs. Barked rope hung coiled against the stage's strouters. An idle fisherman, with a poor-looking face, sat on the stage, his hands slack upon his knees, as he watched green and black shades move through water caught in the play of wind and sunlight.

"Uncle Abe's down with a TB spine. That's why he's dozin' on the wind while his boat's peeling on the beach," Cora said under her breath. "Sure, he should have minded the ways of Uncle Jerry." She looked towards a little man sitting on the stoop of the shed.

Clarissa screwed up her face. She knew that on spring mornings when Uncle Jerry was leaving home to go to his stage, he always grabbed a wooden ladle and went down to the harbour wharf where scummy blubber barrels stood filled with rendered cod liver. He'd dip up a ladleful of the golden liquid, drink it and smack his lips. If he forgot the ladle, he'd stoop to the barrel and slurp a mouthful of cod liver oil. He believed that the smooth oil slipping down his throat would smother any consumption bug that might have gotten inside him.

Cora nodded at Uncle Jerry and remarked, "Sure, 'tis a miracle his white whiskers stay white. But his joints are greased and he's likely got enough energy to jump over the moon on a night when 'tis low."

Across the water, against the hills of St. Anthony, an open door shadowed a fisherman working in an ochre-painted shed. A newly painted boat slapped crimped waters beside a rickety stagehead. Clarissa looked across to Fishing Point, where whales were breaching the waves, then flipping the water with their giant tails and blowing it into the air. Harbour porpoises were chasing a school of herring into the harbour.

The girls came through the orphanage gates, and when they got to the steps, Clarissa pulled her cloth bookbag off her shoulder and laid it on the steps. She sat down beside it for a spell, and looked towards the fence where pink and purple rockets nodded in the breeze. The whole place was being decorated for the prettiest season of all.

Saturday came, and with it stars of sunlight twinkling on the harbour waters. Windows were raised in homes all around the place. The orphanage windows were lifted high, its curtains flapping in warm winds. Birch brooms stirred up dust in every nook and cranny of the orphanage; mattresses were turned and re-cased and pillows beaten out, letting a scattered feather fly.

From around the harbour, women in brin aprons were gathering on the beach to scrub their mats with lye soap in the salty water. Later, they would hurry home with barrows full of clean mats and hang them to dry on wattle fences. The women knew that warm winds sweeping over the land might be chased away at any moment by galing winds with a nasty bite. Sometimes the women had to run and shut their windows, and keep them closed for days.

Although the orphanage grounds were belted by black wrought-iron gates, the fence was open to the mission wharf and beach. Now the children were racing each other down to the wharf. Many of them leaned on the wharf rails, and watched the *Strathcona* sail in with barrels of food in her hold, including whale meat, sealed with reindeer moss, for the huskies. The schooner's deck often held coal for the orphanage furnace, and skinned logs for the construction of houses and fishing rooms. The orphan boys longed to sail out to sea on Dr. Grenfell's thousand pounds of iron: his steel-ribbed steamship.

Clarissa and Cora made their way to the beach to the shouts of boys who had started jigging sculpins from the wharf. When they caught one, they would run after the girls, to touch them with the cold, clammy fish. Imogene squealed and Clarissa smiled, hoping the boys had put a live one down her neck. Peter was coming towards her with his hooked line twined around one hand. When he got close, he opened his other hand and looked at Clarissa. "Here," he said slyly.

She eyed the clear balls on his palm. "What are they?" she asked, as Cora reached over and boldly plucked a ball off his hand.

There was a gleam in his eyes as he said, "They're the balls in fish eyes. First you break the eyeball sac . . ."

"What!" Cora cut him off in disgust. "That's worse than holding a fish doctor!" She tried to let the ball slide off her hand, but it stuck. She shuddered and shook it free.

Clarissa turned back to watch local fishermen boating into the harbour with all sails winged. Gulls waited to lift off the green hills and drop into the harbour for a supper of fish guts.

Soon the harbour was alive with the sounds of boats being moored with iron chains or with thick ropes on the gump posts of the harbour wharf. Before long, men in oilskins were standing at splitting tables, using sharp knives to slit the throats and bellies of codfish. Fish entrails, backbones and heads dropped to the wharf, crowding the men's feet. Fish livers were tossed into oil casks to be rendered into oil.

In a few days, the odour of wet, salt-bulked fish mingled with the sweet scent of wild flowers. Men and women, arms up to their elbows in puncheons full of briny water, washed the fish; then they spread them open on bough-covered wooden flakes to dry. People living near a beach often spread their catch on flat beach rocks. As the fish lay turning into golden leaves in the summer sun, the harbour women sat by a small brook sewing flour bags together for a covering, using string from the bags. The fish would be rounded into piles of rosettes and covered each night – or whenever there was a sign of rain.

Clarissa heard the woman laughing as if they were on a picnic instead of working. She knew they were laughing because the fish would save their winter.

* * *

Late June came like a damp, grey eel, slipping down Clarissa's neck, reminding her of a day last summer when Peter had pushed a long, slimy creature inside her collar after he'd spent the morning on the mission wharf with a hook and line.

Caplin weather, Uncle Aubrey called it. This was the time of year the beach came alive with supple little fish. They rolled into the harbour and up onto the beach in silvery-green waves. Hagdowns pitched on the water in patches almost as thick as the caplin they were dipping for. Harbour dogs danced around the beach, grabbing the caplin flipping around in the sand. Clarissa could hear the husky dogs whining in their kennel. It had been built on the beach so the incoming tide could flush it out. Peter filled a bucket with caplin and went to drop the little fish into the kennel. Other boys were busy gathering caplin in buckets. The caplin would be dried and stored for winter dog food.

All along the road, women were hurrying out of their houses with wash pans to gather fresh caplin for a fry. Poor people came with glad, eager eyes, as if they could hardly wait to rip the white flesh from the backbone of the fish. Clarissa recognized Esther's mother among them.

When Clarissa went into the orphanage through the basement door, Cora's mother was singing in the kitchen, *"I wish, I wish, but all in vain. I wish I were a child, a child again. A child again I shall not be 'til apples grow on an orange tree."*

There were several frying pans going at once on the large coal stove. Clarissa watched as the silvery-green hues of the caplin faded to a crisp brown. The fresh fish would make a good supper.

21
SEESAW AND TRICKS

On rainy days Clarissa stayed inside, not wanting to drabble through mud. The first Saturday morning in July, she looked through the dormitory window at a little cloud hanging all alone in a huge sky. Rain fell, tattering the cloud until it looked like pieces of burst balloon; a sudden blast of sunshine burned it up. Children were soon flooding the grounds with shouts as they lipritty skipped. Clarissa listened to their voices: *"Blue eyes, beauty; grey eyes, greedy guts; brown eyes steal the pudding, fill it with a bunch of fish eyes."*

Clarissa was the last one to go outdoors. Cora was nowhere in sight. As she sat down on one end of the seesaw, she noticed Hipper sauntering towards her. Dr. Grenfell had dropped him at the orphanage, calling him a fine junk of a boy. The other boys nicknamed him Hipper because he had arrived at the orphanage with a bent hipper nail fastening the fly of his overalls. The straps on the overalls were crossed at the back and knotted in the buttonholes of the bib.

"You wanta seesaw?" he called.

Clarissa had never been on the seesaw with anyone but Cora, who kept a slow pace and didn't go too high. The boy's interest in her was a surprise. She reluctantly agreed, leaning on the seesaw with her right forearm and holding on tight with her good hand. Hipper sat on the other end of the seesaw and swung her into the air. She trembled as he seesawed faster and faster, grinning all the while. Then he laughed and stopped suddenly, his feet planted firmly on the ground. Clarissa dangled helplessly in the air. *He is going to do something terrible to me*, she thought just before she felt a sudden shift. Hipper jumped off his end, letting her drop to the ground with a jolt. The braces cut into her legs, making her eyes squinch. Tears trickled down her face as she crawled to her crutches. She wanted to bang the bully with them for knocking her off the seesaw. It was so close to the sloping bank above the beach she could have rolled down over it.

Hipper laughed again. But when Clarissa got up on her crutches and he saw the anger in her eyes, he muttered a threat. "You better keep yer mout' shut or else." Then he took to his heels, running in the direction of Peter, Jakot and the other boys.

Clarissa didn't know what it was about her that brought out the bully in boys. Hipper was as bad as young Ben, who had always seemed quiet and mannerly – until one day last week. He sat down by Clarissa on her locker with a calm look on his face. She had not suspected that his hands were balled. Suddenly he lifted a tight fist and pucked her in the face. Then he ran off, calling back over his shoulder, "Wooden leg!"

"I don't have a wooden leg," she shouted after him.

"You have *two*," he called back.

"And you," she yelled, "have a timber head and the brain of a starfish, which means you're out of luck because a starfish doesn't have a brain."

Cora came out on the veranda laughing as Clarissa came

in from the playground. She looked at Clarissa with a wide grin. "I saw what happened. But bully boys don't always get the best of us. I got Peter good this morning. He was just gonna chop a bit of wood, and I was behind him when he swung the ax over his shoulder. He got me on the forehead, but only a touch. I screamed and fell on the ground. I closed my eyes and never moved a muscle. He let out a big screech and started dancing around crying. 'I arn't killed you, 'ive I?'

"Then he bent down and touched me on the cheek. I opened my eyes real slow. 'Who are you?' I asked. Then I got up and staggered towards the orphanage, leaving him wonderin' if I was gonna drop dead. That's what he gets for plaguing us."

The girls sat on the veranda tossing marbles on their hands and rolling them into their palms; every now and then one of them would laugh as she thought of Cora's trick.

22

NO PICNIC

One morning Clarissa and Cora hurried down the stairs to the kitchen where Cora's mother was slicing bread for a picnic, and hoping aloud that the day would be abroad with sunshine.

"Now, Cora," said Mrs. Payne, "you've a choice between peanut butter sandwiches and strawberry jam sandwiches."

Cora looked at her. "Why can't I have one of each?"

Mrs. Payne shook her head. "No. You've to heed the rules – one or the other."

Clarissa could already taste the gritty peanut butter and the sweetness of berry jam. But she wasn't going on this picnic.

She had gone last year, tailing behind the other children as they galumphed through bramble bushes and willow weeds along the road, squealing and shouting in the morning sunshine. Peter and Jakot, banging on their mouths and hollering, had rushed down the steep bank to where the boat was tied. Clarissa edged her way down, and Uncle Aubrey helped her get from the bank onto the wharf. Then he lifted her into Dr. Grenfell's little rowboat. With Miss Elizabeth sitting in the bow, Jakot and Peter took the boat for its second run to the beach at John's Point. When they got there, the two boys jumped over the prow of the boat and tied the painter to a tree. The children jumped out onto wet sand with shrieks of delight.

Clarissa stayed seated, dismay clouding her face. She'd left her crutches back on the wharf. Miss Elizabeth looked at her without sympathy, "You must remain in the boat, Clarissa. You should not have forgotten your crutches."

Clarissa spent the rest of the day sitting on the cross board. Someday all the orphans would move out into the world and she would be left behind. She tried not to be too down in the mouth, reminding herself that she had God to talk to – and her sister-self. After a while the grounded boat slipped off the sand into the water, and she became mesmerized by its rocking and the warm sun beating down on her. Laughter tumbled into the air as the children kicked balls and played games. Their voices lifted and blended in a familiar rhyme: "*Here we go around the mulberry bush . . .*"

None of the children came to talk with Clarissa as she sat in the boat, her bottom dunch from sitting so long. When Miss Elizabeth brought her a slice of coarse, black bread spread with jam, she was too unhappy to care if she ate it or not. Her stomach was queasy from the heat of the sun and the movement of the boat.

The air cooled, and wind began to stir the water. It rolled over itself towards shore, tickling the rocks and heeling back. *They think I'm so much trouble,* she thought as the children came back, laughing and shouting and jiggling the boat as they got in.

On their way across the harbour, Clarissa let her hand slip over the boat and slide through water. When she pulled it back in, water dripped from her fingertips and fell on Imogene's neck. She jumped, letting out a screech. The boat tipped and water flobbered in over the gunwales. The mistress was quick in admonishing Clarissa, "Be more careful - or else . . ."

When the boat got back to the orphanage wharf, the other children clambered up the wooden ladder. Jakot tossed Clarissa's crutches into the boat. She grabbed them and tried to get a footing, but the braces had cut off her circulation. She was unable to move.

"Get up! I shall never take you again," said Miss Elizabeth crossly.

Clarissa wished Old Keziah would be kinder. She seemed to have wind in her blood, wind that made her tongue snap and whip and rake the children's skin with harsh words. *I'm tough,* Clarissa thought. *I'm not going to cry.* She moved her legs back and forth, and tried a second time to get up. She got to her feet just as Uncle Aubrey came to lift her out of the boat.

* * *

Now the children were on their way to another summer outing. Clarissa followed them down to the bank. Soon Dr. Grenfell's little boat was moving out through the harbour, filled with children going on their summer outing. They might even find some mainderberries. Clarissa's fingers itched to pick the sweet, minty, white berries found in bogs. Her brown eyes brimmed with tears, and she opened them wide, making room so the tears wouldn't fall. She looked longingly after the boat. *I shouldn't have to drag my body as if it were a killick, while everyone else sails free.*

"Hurry!" a voice called from behind her. "If you want to go to the berry grounds and pick blackberries."

Clarissa turned around. "Oh, Cora," she whispered, "you are the *best* of friends."

"I'm really yer only friend," Cora said with a pert look. Clarissa turned on her crutches to follow Cora across the road and down a path to the side of a marsh. Rory was kneeling among the shrubs picking blackberries and eating them. When he saw Cora and Clarissa he hollered, "I'm so full of berries you could crack a nit on me belly."

He'd have to eat a lot, Clarissa thought.

Esther and some of the harbour girls were picking blackberries too. Esther had a baby on her back. She didn't answer when Clarissa called, "Hello." But when Rory started to run around squeezing Smoky Jacks in the girls' faces, turning the air brown, she grabbed him and slapped him on the head.

Clarissa's braces kept her from kneeling in comfort, so she sat by the berry shrubs. She bent towards the marsh to sniff the white flowers of a bog lily. Careful not to disturb the root, she broke it off at the stem, and stuck it in the buttonhole of her sweater. Then she began filling her mouth with blackberries. When she had enough of the small berry, she scooted on her bottom until she reached the overhanging scruff of bog grasses. She went farther and farther into the marsh, trying to find mainderberries. She couldn't find any, and when she started to get to her feet, her crutches sank into a patch of swamp, as soft and wet as fresh dung.

"Come on, Clarissa, before the mudsuckers pull yer under," Cora called.

Clarissa called back: "I have two sticks that can take care of any bog creatures." She laid her crutches flat and dragged herself along on them. By the time she got on her feet, she was drenched. A tiny dog ran up to her and sniffed at the brown patches the peat had made on her dress. The mistresses would scowl and jaw about the mess she was in. Maybe they would punish her. She was so full of berries she didn't care if she didn't get fed.

On the way to the orphanage, the girls stopped by a shallow pond. Clarissa slid to the grass. Then wearing a devil-may-care grin, she unclipped her braces, and unhooked and unlaced her gaiters. Soon she was scooting into the warm water, her dress billowing around her as fluid as a jellyfish. She sat lifting water up on her fingers like threads of gold under the sun. Drops rained from her fingertips like diamonds.

Clarissa turned to the sound of feet scuffing through the grass. She screamed as Jakot, a picnic moocher, grabbed one of her crutches, stuck it through a dry cow platter on the ground and swung it into the air. He dropped the crutch and ran off laughing. Clarissa sat fuming, wishing she could stick his nose through a fresh cow dab and give him freckles that looked like Becky's.

Cora washed the crutch in the pond while Clarissa hurried to put on her gaiters and braces. Then, as Cora stooped to pick a bunch of white field flowers, Peter, who must not have gone on the picnic either, crept up behind her. "Boo!" he shouted. Then he tipped her with his jackboot. "Deadman's flowers! Pick 'em and your father'ill die," he added in a singsong voice.

Cora got up, holding a single flower. "You jockabaun," she shouted, "my father's already dead."

"Well, what else's new about fathers!" Peter exclaimed. "So's mine." He walked away looking as if his hips were walking on their own and his upper body, with his arms tight around it, was along for the ride.

23

YOU HOP LIKE A GRASSHOPPER

Summer brought Clarissa more time to sit on the orphanage steps and read. She had already read *Heidi* to Treffie who was not well enough to learn how to read. Now she was reading Treffie's book again, and savouring the image of Heidi going to the mountains to live with her grandfather.

Peter eyed her as he passed. He went to a corner of the orphanage and scooped a mot in the ground not far from the wall. "I dare you to a game of marbles," he called.

Clarissa closed her book and laid it on the step. She got up with a nod. Today was a good day to pitch marbles. She had been practising: throwing the glass balls against her pillow while the other girls were out playing stick and ball. She wouldn't mind losing some of her marbles, but she didn't want to lose her cat's-eye and her bumblebee. A white-flecked marble and a black one could go.

Cora came around the corner. She shook her head, frowning. "You'll lose 'em all."

Clarissa didn't answer. She sat on the ground and reached into the pocket of her blue gimp. She pulled out the solid-black alley and quickly bazzed it against the orphanage wall. It rebounded close to the hole. She drew in a deep breath as Peter grinned and bazzed his marble. His was closer. He spanned the two marbles with his long, thin fingers; then he grabbed both of them. "Black is for witches," he said. He tossed Clarissa's marble into her lap. "I'll trade you for another one."

"Forget it," she said. She picked up the black marble and dropped it back in her pocket. "I'm not having my bumblebee and my cat's-eye guttled by you."

Peter shrugged just as Cora called excitedly, "Hurry, the WOPS are marching!"

The locals had dubbed the summer volunteers at the Grenfell Mission WOPS (WithOut Pay). They always marched back to St. Anthony Inn with their hands on each other's shoulders, singing in loud, vigorous voices.

Clarissa hurried to be close to the road. She pointed to a tall, handsome fellow and giggled. "He's mine."

Cora pointed to a blond worker, and after a long bout of coughing, she choked, "That one's mine."

Imogene, passing by, rolled her eyes and called, "You can't like these workers. They're too old for you."

"We can, too, Emma Jane. We can like 'em, but we can't love 'em." Cora stuck out her tongue at Imogene.

The girls stood tittering while the workers marched by without a glance their way. Clarissa knew that if a WOP ever spoke to her, her tongue would be like something tied in a knot. Well, maybe a slip-knot, one a little bit of charm could slip her tongue out of.

Clarissa steadied herself on her crutches and bent to grab one of the blue-faced pansies that had sprung from seed blown from Missus Frances's pleasure garden. They were growing in the ditches and along the fence. The sunshine on

Clarissa's arms felt like a caress as she picked the flower locals called "a kiss behind the garden gate." She pressed her lips together, imagining a boy's lips meeting hers. Peter suddenly slapped her bottom; she teetered and then fell to the ground. She scowled up at him, but he was already running away. She shrugged and let her mind wander back to the WOPS.

One night, years before, she and Cora had watched from the top of the stairs as the workers came with Dr. Curtis for a social evening. Miss Brown was one of the mistresses then. She was a mild-mannered American who always dressed like the black of night or the grey of early morning. Even when she wasn't smiling she looked pleasant, her hair swept up and as shiny as a mahogany sideboard under sunlight. That night she breezed in wearing a cameo brooch in a velvet choker on a high-necked green dress that brushed the floor. She didn't look like a mistress and it seemed that she had forgotten *she* was one.

"We drudged all day makin' stringed gauze bags for their coffee beans, and there they are not wanting to put even a cookie crumb on our tongues," Cora complained as the girls watched a covered trolley go by, carrying food for the staff and WOPS. Cora coughed and Miss Brown looked up, but not in time to see Cora. She had scurried out of sight. Clarissa stood there alone.

"Mind that nosiness of yours," the mistress called. Then, with a flick of her hand, she had added, "Now off to bed."

When Miss Brown first came, everyone thought she would be kind all the time because of the full smile on her face. But one day the children started passing the word *damn* from mouth to ear, and it landed in the ears of Tattle-tale Imogene, who rushed it to the ears of the mistress. Miss

Brown let Imogene spell the bad word, stopping her before she got to the *n*. Those children tattled on for using blaighard were lined up and lye soap brushed on their tongues with a large brush and then lathered. They were left with closed mouths for a full minute and then their mouths were rinsed. Peter claimed he had only said *beaver's dam*; anyway, he always brushed his teeth with soap, so it was all the same to him.

The children had found it hard to forgive Miss Brown for putting something into their mouths that was even worse than the morning porridge.

Clarissa forgave the mistress because she was generally kind. One summer day when the other children had gone berry picking and Clarissa was stuck in the orphanage by herself, Miss Brown gave her a doll and cradle.

Clarissa turned from her thoughts of Miss Brown and the WOPS. She got to her feet, looking around to make sure Peter wasn't back. Then she went to sit on the orphanage steps. She fingered the marbles in her pocket listlessly, no longer interested in games or reading. She looked up to see Uncle Aubrey, who was taking care of Dr. Grenfell's greenhouse. He called her to come to the summer vegetable garden. Early in June, Clarissa and the other children had dropped seeds into trenches made in freshly-turned ground. She had imagined carrots too small to see wrapped inside them. Rain softening the seeds' skins and the pull of the sun would help the carrots grow, pushing their roots out beneath the ground and their leaves up above it.

Clarissa followed the caretaker to the little garden. Her face broadened into a smile. It was as if a magician had cast a green spell. Lacy carrot leaves had popped above the earth. Beside them, lettuce stood in rows like green flowers.

Clarissa's mouth watered at the thought of eating fresh lettuce with sugar and vinegar falling through it on a hot day. It would be as good as biting into ice crystals from an iceberg.

A warm breeze lifted Clarissa's hair as she made an unsteady gait back to the orphanage. She turned at the sound of heavy footsteps. Dr. Grenfell was coming up the walkway behind her, in a heavy sweater and hip boots. He stopped to swing Teddy, a new, bare-legged orphan, up on his shoulders. Clarissa looked down, relieved that high gaiters hid the sight of her legs, even if it was too hot for them.

Dr. Grenfell dropped Teddy to the lawn with a laugh, and the little boy ran off. Then the doctor walked to where Clarissa had stopped. Leaning forward with his hands on his knees, he said lightly, "You hop around like a grasshopper. We'll need to adjust your braces."

Clarissa looked at the fatherly, tanned face of the doctor, his hair and mustache almost as white as snow, and returned his smile. Her smile faded as he went ahead of her into the orphanage. She looked towards the other children running and playing. Providence had saved the doctor's words from falling on their ears; otherwise, the nickname Grasshopper would have stuck to her like fish slime as long as she was at the orphanage.

She had always seen Dr. Grenfell as a kind man, sometimes even a god who had stooped low enough to touch the common people. Now she wanted to yell at him, "Grasshopper – one of the creepy, long-legged creatures Peter put down my neck, and me with my hands on two crutches."

Clarissa replayed the doctor's words in her mind, and then muttered them aloud, adding, "I do well to hop around like a grasshopper, seeing I have two legs and a grasshopper has four."

She sat down and let herself fall back on the stubbly grass, tears streaming down her face. She felt heavy, as if the Atlantic Ocean was getting inside her, filling her up – drowning her! *I am not an orphan and I shouldn't have to feel like one,* she thought miserably. *It's bad enough that some orphans treat me as if I'm different, but not the doctor too!* She cried harder.

"What's wrong, Clarissa?" Cora was running towards her, looking anxious. "You're crying so much, your eyelashes are sticking to your face."

"Dr. Grenfell thinks I hop like a grasshopper!"

"Well, *he* can't do that," Cora answered lightly, plopping down beside her.

The girls looked at each other and burst out laughing at the idea of Dr. Grenfell hopping.

When they stopped, Cora reasoned, "It was just a remark. Sure, there's nothin' to be made of it. It was likely a thought gone as soon as it was said."

"It will never be gone from *my* mind," Clarissa retorted, "not even when I'm eighty-five and lying in bed doing naughty things like smoking."

Cora screwed up her face and shook her head adamantly. "I'll never smoke. Look at a stove when it smokes. Sure, its insides are darker than a bark pot. Anyway, you should be so lucky to live until yer eighty-five." Her voice trailed off. "I might not live that long."

Clarissa avoided her last remark. "Look!" she said, pointing to an insect on a blade of grass. "Insects aren't so scary. That one's tinier than the slip of grass it's on." She leaned down for a closer look. "Its wings are so thin you can't see them until the insect dances on the leaf, its legs like lines of gold embroidery thread. Look at the tail! Nothing more than a long, black thread."

"It's liable to have a grand name we can't spell or pronounce," said Cora. "And mind what God said about humans. We're the same as grasshoppers. Sure, 'tis in the Bible."

"I don't believe so," Clarissa said scornfully, pulling herself to her feet.

"Well, it is then. Reverend Penny preached on it the Sunday you were sick. He got it from the old prophet Isaiah. 'Tis thinking you're doin' while the reverend's preaching. Sure, there's the little girl in the Bible who was taken far away from her home to the house of Naaman the leper, and a little boy was crippled when his nurse dropped him. Then there's Jesus. He loved children even more than Dr. Grenfell loves them. He said it was better for someone to have his neck weighed with a rock and drowned than for him to hurt children."

"You're a thoughtful soul with a good memory," Clarissa said, her face relaxing into a smile.

Cora frowned. "Treffie will soon be no more than a soul. Today, while you were dusting the staff's quarters, Missus Frances took her to see Dr. Curtis at the hospital. I heard Housemother Budden say Treffie's not long for this world. Sure, 'tis up to three o'clock and the Missus went just after breakfast."

Clarissa knew that Treffie had been in the isolation room on the third floor of the orphanage all by herself for a long time. She had sneaked in once to see her. Treffie had turned her thin, white face. In a pitiful, weak voice she gasped, "The coughs come quick, Clarissa. You better leave before you gets a rattle on yer chest."

Clarissa had tried to comfort the little girl. "You'll soon be a soul with wings that will take you to your mother and father."

Treffie's dull eyes lightened. Then they closed. The only

sound in the room was Clarissa's crutches, thumping across the floor as she left her friend behind.

* * *

Clarissa was looking through her dormitory window a few days into the second week of Treffie's hospital stay when she saw Uncle Aubrey pulling a cart across the road. It held a painted white box tapered at both ends. It looked like a dead box.

Clarissa imagined Treffie flying away like an angel, finding a cloud to sit on and drift towards Heaven, towards her mother. Still, Clarissa felt as if an icicle had slipped inside her heart as she went to find Cora.

Cora sobbed quietly as the girls went to the kitchen to tell Cora's mother. She didn't seem surprised.

"The dear child had a poor destiny," Mrs. Payne said with a sigh. "She lost her father and mother in one year. The father went trappin', and when he didn't come home, Treffie's mother took sick and died. Treffie was left in the little cottage with her dead mother. The poor little thing covered her with sealskins, thinkin' she'd wake up if she was warm. Dr. Grenfell told us that when he found Treffie, she was standin' on the headland as still as a figurehead. Her yellow dress, one he had brought her on his mission the year before, was flickerin' in the wind like candlelight." Mrs. Payne looked into the girls' miserable faces and assured them, "Now Treffie's safe in the arms of Jesus. She won't be lonely or in pain anymore."

* * *

Clarissa, her mind knocked astray by the loss of Treffie, spent a lot of time looking through her dormitory window. One day

Missus Frances, passing by the open door, called to her, "Off with you – get out and enjoy the day. None of us has a hold on life that cannot be forced from our grip."

"But I can't help thinking about Treffie," Clarissa murmured.

"Thinking when you can be doing, Child, makes for time lost to idleness."

"I don't want to be doing. If I don't stop and think about Treffie, she'll be gone."

Missus Frances came close to her and said gently, "As long as you have a mind you can use it to remember, but your hands can still be busy. Trophenia does not need her body anymore. Death brings only a change to life, not an end. Your baby body changed to accommodate your older one. All of our bodies change throughout their lives, and although what happens after we die is a mystery, we know death isn't the end of us."

Clarissa nodded, and Missus Frances left the room.

Cora came into the room. "I'm going to get some forget-me-not seeds from Uncle Aubrey. We'll have flowers next year for Treffie."

"I'll go with you," Clarissa offered.

* * *

Uncle Aubrey was quick to get the girls seeds and a shovel, and Cora dug a small trench inside the orphanage fence. Clarissa dropped in a seed for each letter in Treffie's name. Cora looked at Clarissa and dropped seven seeds in beside hers, saying, "God rested on the seventh day." Clarissa nodded and Cora covered the double portion of seeds. She sprinkled the ground with water brought in a can from the lobby.

Clarissa went back inside the orphanage trying not to think of her little friend as being in the ground. She brightened. *If flowers and carrots can sprout out of the earth, Treffie's life can sprout too – somewhere.*

24
BARRED OUT

Clarissa was playing cobby house alone by the snout of a yellow birch tree close to the beach. She missed Cora, who had a bout of summer sickness and was staying close to the orphanage toilets. When the first lunch bell rang, Clarissa dropped hers and Cora's collection of seashells and chainies in a hollow at the base of the tree, and pulled a flat rock over it. She pulled herself to her feet and slipped the crutches under her armpits. She tried to hurry along the path, so she could wash up and get to the table before the second bell rang, but her braces held her back. There wasn't a sign of anyone when she reached the orphanage. The second bell was already ringing. She got her breath; then she turned the handle on the basement door. It wouldn't open.

"I can't be barred out!" she groaned just as a raindrop fell on her nose. She steadied herself and rattled the handle with her good hand. She knocked and waited, sorry now that she hadn't gone around to the front door. She listened for noises coming from inside, but the only sound she heard came from a sudden torrent of rain beating down on her. It filled her eyes and dripped into her open mouth. She looked at the window beside the door, clenched her hand, and, pulling her sleeve down over her knuckles, she let her fist fly at the long, narrow windowpane. Shards of glass fell with a clatter onto the wooden floor inside. She stood quietly, rain and tears mingling.

Through the broken window, Clarissa caught a glimpse of Imogene running down the stairs. She unlocked the door and opened it. Her eyebrows lifted at the sight of Clarissa shivering on the steps. Then, without saying a word, she let the door slam shut. Clarissa pushed the unlocked door open and stumbled inside, fuming at the sight of Imogene running up the stairs. The mistresses would soon know about the window from Tattle-tale Imogene.

Clarissa hobbled upstairs to the hall and stood there streaming wet, her stomach growling like an angry husky. No one would care that she had not eaten since breakfast; no one would notice that her knuckles were bleeding. She dragged off her coat and was hanging it in the hallway to dry when she saw Miss Elizabeth hurrying towards her.

"You are not in time for lunch, so you will not have supper either." Miss Elizabeth snapped her mouth shut; it took on its familiar pursed shape.

Missus Frances, coming out from the dining room, overheard the younger woman. "Clarissa missed her lunch. She will not go to bed without her supper, even if it is one slice of bread."

Clarissa warmed to Missus Frances for taking up for her. Mean feelings towards the mistresses made her teeth tighten and grind together like agitated ice pans. As soon as a mistress treated her well, her whole body settled.

Miss Elizabeth's voice softened as she lowered it. "If we don't punish you, the other girls will pick on you."

They were interrupted by Dr. Curtis, coming into the

orphanage from the basement. "Who broke the window?" he asked sternly.

Miss Elizabeth answered: "Clarissa, *your* pet, did that. I've been told it was an accident."

The doctor lifted one dark eyebrow. He didn't say a word as he went towards the library. The mistress looked at Clarissa. "You must be his pet. He didn't deny it."

Clarissa didn't know how she could be his pet. She hardly ever saw him. Sometimes he was with Dr. Grenfell when her legs were being examined, but he was never friendly. Still, he didn't seem angry about the window and, if her luck held, she wouldn't be punished for breaking it. Clarissa wondered if Imogene had explained the break as an accident, so she wouldn't be blamed for locking the basement door.

She started up the stairs, stopping when she heard whispering beside the staircase. She couldn't see anyone, but when she got to the second floor, she heard girls' voices raised in a chant. *"Bay Girl, Bay Girl, come to supper: two cods' heads and a lump of butter."*

She was sure one of the girls was Imogene.

25

A FALL IN SUMMER

The first weeks of summer were almost too wonderful to bear, especially those mornings when the dormitory room had pooled with sunshine by the time the breakfast bell rang.

One morning after breakfast, Clarissa swung herself down the steps of the orphanage, and out towards the garden by the barns. She listened to cows lowing and horses whinnying. Leaves, wrapped in warm and gentle sunshine, soughed in the breeze.

She turned to see Jakot and Owen lumbering up from the beach with seashells and sand for the coopy house. When the hens ate sand and pieces of seashell, their eggshells were hard and didn't crack in the hands of children collecting them from nests of hay. One wily hen had managed to fly off the ground and land in the lettuce patch which it pecked full of holes. It was clucking against Peter's chest as he clipped its wings. Clipping the wings was Uncle Aubrey's way of dealing with flighty hens.

Clarissa made her way down the beach path. Girls and boys were standing on the low rail of the mission wharf; their arms hung over the top rail as they looked down into the clear water. On the beach beside the wharf, children were blowing up sculpins by hitting them across the stomach with a stick. Young Ben went from breaking seaweed bubbles to teasing a starfish with a twig, getting it to crawl to a rotting caplin alive with flies. Its points closed over the caplin, and the starfish became a ball. It went limp, and then flat as it died under Ben's foot.

Clarissa watched children skipping flat stones across the water without making a splash, trying to finish a rhyme before the stones sank: "*A duck and drake and a tatey, pork cake . . .*"

It was getting close to lunchtime; Clarissa felt tired and hungry. She went back to the orphanage and sat on the concrete wall outside the building. She watched children playing hopscotch and lallick, running, jumping, swinging – moving freely without sticks. Their feet had worn a path through the grass to a set of swings set up in the yard by Dr. Grenfell and Uncle Aubrey. Clarissa's brown eyes almost turned green with envy at the sight of Cora and Imogene on the swings. She would sit on a swing if her left hand was strong enough to hold on, and her feet were able to push her. She wanted to be swinging high and higher, until her feet were hanging in the sky. There were days she wished she were a puffin on the wing.

She closed her eyes, moving her body back and forth, imagining she was swinging through the air. Her eyes flew open as she lost her balance and fell back over the concrete wall to the flat alley below; her braces and crutches clattered like broken bones as she hit the hard ground. The brutal pain in her head was aggravated by the familiar ring of the lunch bell. The other children ran laughing towards the orphanage. Some of them looked her way, but they didn't stop. She didn't blame them. They wanted their lunch, and they needed ten minutes to get inside and wash up before the next bell.

Clarissa lay feeling woolly headed, waiting for the pain to subside. After a while she put her fingers on her head. It was still together. She knew it would be, just as it had been the other times when she had fallen. Last summer she had hit her head on the leg of the table in the lunchroom. A week after that she bumped her head against the radiator in the dormitory. The cut had bled onto her navy sweater with the red trim.

The pain lessened and Clarissa got her hands on her crutches and pulled herself up. She tried to ignore the heaviness of her body and the discomfort of the knobby handles of the crutches in her armpits as she dragged herself up the steps to the orphanage. The second bell was like a tongue banging her ears. When she was finally inside the lunchroom, the children looked at her with pity. Missus Frances didn't ask how she was or tell her to wash up, but her voice was kind, "I think you had better go to bed; I'll send you something to eat."

Despite the pain, Clarissa managed to haul her body up the stairs and into the dormitory. She undressed slowly, dropping her clothes across the bed. She pulled her nightgown over her head and got into bed, feeling stunned. Soon Missus Frances came with food: apple salad with savoury dressing. It was the first time Clarissa had seen staff food. She had always wondered what was on the covered trolley. She would tell the other girls about the apple salad.

Clarissa rested in bed the next day, not getting up except to go to the toilet. For the next two days she stayed in the dormitory, her head so heavy she didn't even want to eat. Missus Frances brought her food for the next three days. Each time she cast a critical eye over her patient, exclaiming, "Clarissa, you *must* be more careful!"

From the window, Clarissa watched the other children playing games. They ran into the wind lifting light, energetic arms. It was all so wonderful - the things they could do.

I'll do all that someday, she vowed.

26
A SAVAGE ATTACK

Clarissa was lying across her bed reading *Little Women* when she heard screaming in the distance. She shrugged it off, thinking that some rascal – Peter most likely – had put a spider in someone's ear, the same as he had done to her last year. The screaming became more intense, and then stopped. She grabbed her crutches and hopped to the window: children and adults were running in the direction of the beach. *Probably just a fight,* she thought, and went back to lie on her bed. She picked up her book and was deep into reading when Cora burst into the room panting, strangling the words she was trying to get out. "Peter . . . dogs!"

"Peter," said Clarissa in a dismissive tone, "should go where the dogs don't bark."

Cora's eyes widened in horror; Clarissa dropped her book, and its pages swished shut. Something was wrong. Cora never put a face on her like this; her eyes looked ready to fall out of their sockets.

Cora wrung out her words, her hands clasped: "He's lying on the ground, bitten into and streaked with blood. Dead!"

The last word came like a hammer. Clarissa's head seemed to crack with the blow. Her face and eyes grew heavy; her heart felt like a rock.

Cora fell across her bed, whimpering, "I wished him dead."

Clarissa looked at her best friend. "But it wasn't that kind of dead," she said slowly. "I wanted to bat him so many times with my crutches, and I would have if I could have stood without them." Now she wished she could have saved him from the wild teeth of the dogs. He must have felt the same kind of pain that bit into her hip and foot long after Dr. Grenfell had split her tendons and sewn up her skin.

"Besides," she added hopefully, "you don't know if he's *really* dead."

"Yes I do. Uncle Aubrey threw whale meat in the kennel to get the dogs off him; then he dragged him out and put his finger against his neck. He looked up and said, in a strange voice, 'This boy ain't needin' salve and bandages. His breath's gone.'"

Cora's eyes were downcast. "No one seemed to know what Peter was doin' in the kennel."

"Maybe he was hanging off the kennel fence and the dogs dragged him in." Clarissa thought of all the times she'd seen Peter locking his heels on fences and dropping his head, his arms dangling, while the younger orphans watched him with open mouths.

The sound of gunshots drew the girls' attention to the window. They looked at each other. Now the huskies were dead, too.

Missus Frances warned the children at suppertime, as she had done many times before, not to go near husky dogs. "They have a savage nature like the wolves that are part of their ancestry. From the wolves they get their howl and whine. Remember," the mistress cautioned, "dogs will lick your hand today and eat you tomorrow. They are as deceitful as wolves who, trappers will tell you, are not dead until their teeth show. As long as their lips are together, they have enough life to bite. There has been trouble with dogs in St. Anthony before this. Arms and legs – and faces – have been bitten into and torn. The dogs have to be destroyed after an attack. Once they taste human blood, they don't stop until they get flesh."

The mistress lifted her chin, her voice grave. "After today we will not speak of Peter's mishap. Someone else will soon take his place at the table." Her eyelashes flittered as if flicking away tears.

That night, the silence from the kennel was more lonely than the dogs' howls had been. The girls in Clarissa's dormitory slipped quietly into their beds and fell asleep without a word. Clarissa awoke to the lonely sound of galing winds. She stirred, relieved that although the wind howled like huskies, it couldn't get inside. The wind used to whip around the old orphanage, looking for open seams in the green wood. Sometimes the wind had a tongue of rain; Clarissa would wake to cold, damp air breathing in her face.

She fell back asleep and dreamed about Peter. *He and other children are outside the dog kennel hussing the animals. Some boys dare Peter to climb over the galvanized mess wire and jump into the kennel with the four husky dogs. Jakot is grinning. "If you can do that without showing you're afraid, the huskies won't attack yer." Peter is acting cocky, but fear surfaces in his eyes as he drops into the kennel. They widen at the bared, white teeth of the dogs. The animals turn on him, fur straight up on their backs, their tails bristling and*

*their jowls foaming. Peter's heavy pants are ripped from him
and blood drips from torn, white skin into the sawdust-cov-
ered ground. Clarissa balances herself on one crutch and
pushes the other through a hole in the wire kennel and hits
one, two, three, four dogs on their heads. They lift their
snouts into the air and howl as if they are wolves baying at the
moon. Then they run to cower in the corner. Peter crawls
away whimpering; the dogs come back after him. Clarissa
hears him screaming; she's afraid the dogs will leave Peter,
leap the fence and turn on her. The screaming stops; she's
too scared to look back. The other children go shrieking
towards the orphanage. Clarissa tries to follow them, but
huskies catch a whiff of her blood from the monthly eggs broken inside her. They leap the fence and attack her. She falls
down knowing she will never get away until the huskies have
eaten her legs.* She awoke from her dream, her heart pounding. Peter was really dead!

The next morning, Clarissa overheard the older boys
talking outside the orphanage about Peter and the blood on
the ground in the kennel. She wanted to dream Peter alive
so she could say she was sorry for thinking he was mean –
even though he was – and for not believing him when he
said his people came from Norse warriors – even if they
didn't.

She remembered Peter telling Miss Ellis, in a proud
voice, about his father and Norsemen. Clarissa had expected
the school ma'am to give him a poke with her ruler, and call
him fanciful, but she hadn't. She looked at him as if anything
was possible. She said she had heard of a Newfoundland his-
torian – a man named W. A. Munn – who was writing a book
suggesting that Vikings had once lived near St. Anthony. "No
one knows the many bloodlines in this country," the school

ma'am had answered, as if upholding Peter's belief that he
came from Viking blood. Peter had looked around at the rest
of the children with a bold and lofty look on his face.

* * *

"It is important to feel you belong to someone," Clarissa murmured to Cora as they sat together at the funeral service.

Cora looked at Clarissa. "Peter was good on times," she
admitted reluctantly. She turned her head towards the pulpit,
where Reverend Penny was about to start his sermon.

Reverend Penny assured everyone that the dogs had only
hurt Peter's body, which was just a box holding his life. They
had freed him to go up to God. The Reverend's voice rose
solemnly. "We must not think of a person as being dead. Peter
is gone away from a torn body into the garden of God. In
Heaven he has a new life. He will be there with his mother and
father. We all have to pay the debt of nature someday."

Debt! Clarissa never thought of herself as owing her
breath to anyone. She thought it was a gift. It had not occurred
to her until now that her body would go into a pitty hole someday. Jakot, Owen, Hipper and Simon looked as mournful as
the black bands on their left arms, as they each reached for a
handle of the barrow under the white box holding Peter. They
carried it out of the church.

Clarissa and Cora walked together down the road to the
graveyard. An old fisherman, standing there, watching and
puffing on his TD pipe, said, as if to himself, "These are dog
days: July and August. The Dog Star, the brightest star in the
night sky, rises and sets with the sun, and no one knows what
effect this could have on wild dogs." He went down the road
shaking his head.

Thinking of Peter barred inside a box reminded Clarissa of the other box up on Tea House Hill. She wondered if she and Cora would ever have the nerve to pry up the cover. Closed boxes seemed to hold dead things. Her face brightened. Or treasures.

A cloud crossed her face. She shouldn't be thinking about treasures with Peter just dead. Guilt settled inside her.

27

NEWS ABOUT GOING HOME

Clarissa had been twelve for six months when Missus Frances called her into the office. She stood, leaning on her crutches, wondering what awful thing she had done now.

"Your mother has written to us," the woman said quickly. "She has sent for you to come home."

Clarissa's eyes widened. Her voice came out in a hoarse whisper. "My mother wants me to come home." Her body swayed as if an earthquake had started beneath her feet.

Going home had been her daydream and her night dream through the long years, sustaining her through every hard blow. But now, sitting in the office looking across the desk at Missus Frances, her concept of home fled as swiftly as if it were a dream she had awakened from. An icy feeling swept through her.

"Your mother feels it is time for you to be instructed in the Roman Catholic faith."

"Did she say . . . uh . . .?" Clarissa couldn't finish her sentence under the probing eyes of the mistress.

"Yes?" The woman's lips pulled tight as she waited for Clarissa to finish.

Clarissa drew in a deep breath. "Did she say she missed me?"

"Now, Child, why would she tell me that? You've been gone for most of your life. You may not have been missed, but you are wanted home."

Clarissa wasn't sure what to think, what to say, what to feel. She had wanted so much to go home, praying the Protestant way to get there. She had never been a real orphan; now she wouldn't have to be a Protestant either.

"You came here because your parents were concerned about your health. You were kept here at Dr. Grenfell's request. You are going home because your mother is concerned about your religious instruction. Likely there will be many adjustments to be made on both sides. Understand, Clarissa, that you will be going home to an outhouse and a water bucket and a galvanized tub for bathing. Though your family has social and economic standing in the community, the place itself is backward. You will not have the privileges you have enjoyed here."

Missus Frances turned the pages of a file in front of her. It was from the orphan logbook. "Let's see what has been written about you: '. . . a fair-skinned child with chestnut hair and brown eyes.'

"You came to the Grenfell Hospital in 1915, where you were treated for infantile paralysis. You were home once. That was in 1917 when you were four, and Dr. Grenfell was away. When he returned, he wrote a letter asking your mother to send you back to the hospital. Let me see. Yes, here it is. You were brought back in 1918, when you were five. That was in the last year of the war. It was a strange time to send a child away; torpedoes could be anywhere.

"On October 18, 1920, you came to the orphanage from

the hospital. You will like to hear what else has been written about you. 'She is very meek towards older people. An obedient child – gets on remarkably well. She has won the affection of the staff by her responsiveness and courage. She is a very bright child and good in school. She helps around the orphanage. Clarissa is very good-looking.'"

Clarissa looked at the mistress. "They . . . *you* think that about me?" she whispered. "That's how I am seen? I wish I had known that all these years. I thought I was in everyone's way." To herself she added, *If I had known anyone thought I was smart and good-looking, I would have been nicer to myself in the mirror.*

"You never complained." The mistress's voice was gentle.

But I did inside. There were times I wanted to squeeze the sides of Miss Elizabeth's face together until her eyes were back to back, making her nose look as long as a rat's tail.

She suddenly felt an attachment she wanted to hold on to. There was no such place as home outside the orphanage. She was familiar with this place and the people around her, even if she didn't like all of them.

Missus Frances sighed and looked at Clarissa. "You are only one child among many who have passed through this place. But you have stood out from the other children in many ways. You must know, Clarissa, that life in a place such as this doesn't always go the way you want it to, but in a family there is the same reality. Harsh times can stand out like the black spot on a sheet of white paper. Despite its imperfections, Grenfell's Mission has saved numerous lives."

Missus Frances paused, and then continued, "Everyone here is different. Becky gets made fun of for her freckles.

Johnny has ears like jug handles and his tongue is long enough to lick the sleepy men out of his own eyes. Harold is so slothful he couldn't earn the salt for his porridge. Other children have problems you don't know about. Most of our children have suffered in one way or another."

"But I am different in a way that hurts. Freckles and big ears don't keep other children from running. I want to be normal!"

"You have to think of the things you can do. Your mind is not crippled by mental drawbacks as some children's are. It dances with spirit, and it runs free to take you places many of the other children will never go."

"My mind?" Clarissa asked, as if she hadn't thought about her mind as an asset, like a healthy limb.

"Reading has opened up the world for you. You can go back in time to visit Joan of Arc, the courageous Maid of Orleans, as she gallops into battle. You can stay in the present and read about the place where the Simms boys from St. Anthony went to war and gave their lives to save others. Your world is not limited. It is only different like Helen Keller's. There are no birds singing and no human voices in her ear and she cannot see the world as you can. Helen freed herself from her disabilities by concentrating on her capabilities. She set herself free to travel around the world, first in her mind and now in her body. Despite being blind and deaf, she was graduated from one of the most prestigious universities in the United States. You will learn more of that woman, I'm sure. Maybe you will meet her someday."

"I'd like to meet her and The Statue of Liberty!" Clarissa exclaimed, letting out a gasp at the possibility of seeing a beautiful lady, her raised hand holding a flaming torch high in the sky. She often wished there was such a statue here, like a lighthouse, out on the point. "Someday," she said with conviction, "I will sail into New York Harbour and see the Statue of Liberty, all one hundred and fifty-two feet of her!"

"It isn't so far away," the mistress said encouragingly. She stood up and came around to touch Clarissa's shoulder. "You have been here long and you have suffered much. But now you are going home to a family who was willing to give you up to the care of Dr. Grenfell for your sake."

Clarissa lifted hopeful eyes to the mistress, glad she was taking time to talk with her. She asked breathlessly, "I will get better – I will be able to walk like my brothers and sisters, won't I?" She was sure someone had told her that when she finished growing up she would get better. She had been long-ing, waiting to be like other people, to be so well her body would forget she ever had paralysis.

The mistress shook her head. "You will never walk on your own. Someday you may even need a chair with wheels to take the weight off your body. Knowing you, Clarissa, you will be going down hills with your brakes open."

"A wheelchair!" Clarissa gasped, her eyes like bright moons that dark clouds were passing over. Her chest rose and fell rapidly as she struggled to breathe against the mistress's words, hope nipped in a small place near her heart. "You mean my limbs are damaged for good?" Her voice was bare-ly above a whisper.

"Damaged, Child, but not for good or bad."

Other children got better when Dr. Grenfell was finished with them. Her eyes flooded with tears. Missus Frances was saying she would have to give up her one great dream. She let her head drop into her arms.

The mistress didn't know what it was like to walk with crutch knobs twisting in her armpits, her legs in pain, her left hand weak. She had never had to stand out from everyone else as "the cripple." *Someday I will be better,* Clarissa thought stubbornly. Her spirit rose inside her like a flame, blowing out the darkness of the mistress's words.

That night Clarissa lay in bed unable to sleep. Moonlight shone through the long window, making a beam across the room, illuminating the faces of Imogene and the other girls sound asleep. *Harmless looking until their tongues rear and hiss,* she thought spitefully.

She would miss the land beside the big ocean which sometimes rolled and stretched like a kitten in the sun; other times it arched its back and hissed like a tomcat under ships riding on it. She hoped it would be gentle on her way back to her real home.

She finally fell asleep, and into dreams. *Treffie is shooting through the sky like a Northern Light; she goes through a hole cut out of the dark sky by a bright star. On the other side of the sky, a gentle-faced woman takes her hand. Treffie smiles up at her mother.* That dream ended and another one began. *Peter is lying on the ground bleeding. A red slab of skin torn away from his face lies beside him. Huskies growl and bite at Clarissa's crutches as she stumbles past Peter's body. Someone takes Peter away. The dogs are shot. Clarissa ventures back to the empty kennel. Steadying her crutches, she reaches to pick up a piece of flint lying in the dirt. The dogs must have chewed off the sealskin string that had held it around Peter's neck.*

Clarissa awoke with her nails digging into her palm. She opened her hand, expecting to see the flint. Her empty palm showed four crescents marked by her fingernails. For some reason she thought then of the brass-sheeted box on Tea House Hill. She knew she would have to go back there before she went away.

28
PREPARING FOR HOME

"Come on. Off with you to the hospital," Miss Elizabeth called to Clarissa after her breakfast the next morning. "You will have a vaccination for diphtheria and get fitted with new braces. Now let me see that smile of yours."

Clarissa's heart leaped in trepidation. *It must be true; I'm going home! I'll have to tell Cora.*

Miss Elizabeth opened the front door to the orphanage and Clarissa swung past her, trying to be careful as she went down the steps. If she broke a leg she'd be put in the infirmary. She would never forget the time a disease had spread among the harbour residents, and all the children in the orphanage had to be inoculated against it. She had not minded having her back punched with a needle. But that night she had awakened with the urge to vomit. She made it to the toilet and back to bed. She slid down on her mattress and back to sleep, despite a rowdiness in her stomach. When she awoke the next morning, she realized that she had messed her bed. The other girls, holding their noses, went off to breakfast. Soon Miss Elizabeth came in with a tight face. Without saying a word, she took the dirty sheet off the bed, folded it into a rope and wrapped it around Clarissa's waist. The mistress ordered her to sit on the floor. Then she tied her to the leg of the bed with the ends of the sheet.

Clarissa had leaned against the bed frame, too sick to undo the sheet. Not long after, Missus Frances came and untied her. After she left, Clarissa was not well enough to put on her braces. She crawled into the bath and toilet room, dragged herself to the toilet, and threw up. Dora, a young helper, tapped on the door and came in. "You poor orphan," was all she said as she helped Clarissa into the bathtub.

Clarissa shook her head to scatter the memories of things that were behind her, as she reached the doors of the hospital and struggled to get inside. She was sitting in the waiting room when Dr. Curtis came in. "Hello," he said briskly. He called her into a small room where he quickly gave her a vaccination shot and fitted her with new braces. He dismissed her without saying anything about her going home. She left the hospital, feeling so awkward in her new braces, she was afraid of falling on her face.

It took her a long time to get to the orphanage. She began to cry as she tried to get up the steps. She sat down and looked at her red skin, chafed and well on its way to being worn through by the new braces. She stood up, leaning against her crutches, and started back to the hospital. When she finally got to the front hall of the building, Dr. Curtis was coming out of one of the wards. She took a deep breath and called, "Dr. Curtis, my braces hurt."

Without looking at her, he snapped, "I have no time for you."

She tried to console herself. *He's busy with all the patients. That's why he's sharp with me.* Then she felt a surge of self-pity. *A lot of these people haven't had pain for as long as I have.*

Some of them will die, said a voice inside her head.

She sat down on a bench, thinking she would like to see Dr. Curtis walking on crutches with his legs in braces for a day. She was still there, tears falling from her eyes, when the doctor came through the hall an hour later. He nodded for her to follow him into the examination room. "Your braces are too long," he admitted. "I'll shorten them a bit." After he was satisfied with his work, he took her hand and said in a gentle voice, "Goodbye."

Dr. Grenfell's words, *You hop around like a grasshopper,* echoed through her head to the beat of her crutches on the corridor floor. Her mind was a fierce self arguing against a body she didn't want, as she tried to swing legs that felt heavier than ever. The hobble back to the orphanage seemed to take forever; her lame left hand felt too tired to hold the crutch steady. Finally she was inside the familiar building. She went to the dining room and sat in her seat at the head of the table, her crutches beside her. She stared at the long, empty table, thinking about her life as an orphan, remembering Treffie and Peter. Other children's faces came to her, but she tried to believe she would miss only Cora. She lifted her bottom off the seat, got on her crutches and went past the closed doors of the mistresses' quarters.

I don't want to leave, she decided. *The only family I know is here.* The strange, far-off place Missus Frances called Clarissa's home was a shadow; her family was part of a dream she had a long time ago.

She left the orphanage and followed the path down the grassy bank to a dark wooden shelter; shafts of daylight poured up between the planks in the floor. Peter and the other orphan boys used it for their camp. She made her way from there to the beach, and stood looking at it as if seeing it for the first time. Tinkling water dappled shale, and smooth, round rocks scattered as if by a mighty, sweeping sea. Beside the wharf the briny sea played the ropes that held little boats.

Clarissa made her way back to the orphanage and sat on the veranda. *No dancing. Not ever. I will always be like this. No, not even like this. I will be in a wheelchair.* Her lower lip dropped; tears rolled down her cheeks and fell into her mouth. She kept her eyes wide open, willing herself not to blink, not to care – to become a statue. Her eyes fastened on an island of ice out in the bay. Saddleback gulls and Irish Lords hovered over the iceberg. They settled on it for a moment. Then they winged their way above it, as if blessing it on its journey around the coves of the island of Newfoundland.

Missus Frances came outside. "Come on. We have a job to do. You have to be outfitted for home." One eyebrow lifted like a soft, light feather. "Your mother is going to have a time combing out the clits in that thick hair of yours, if you keep the habit of blowing on the pussy willows. You have them caught in your hair like burrs."

Clarissa dragged her body up the stairs to the big clothing storeroom. *I've been missed from my mother's heart and her arms. I know I have.* She had flung those words into her pillow more than once, remembering vaguely her mother's tears on her face when she had been sent back to the orphanage. She burst into tears, dropped her crutches and fell into Missus Frances's arms – arms familiar to her eyes, yet strange to touch.

"Now, now," the mistress chided. "Think of all the children here who would like to have their own flesh and blood family." She bent to pick up Clarissa's crutches. "We've no time to waste. We must pick through the clothes donated by our American friends so you can be fitted out and sent home."

Clarissa always wore donated dresses. The navy one with red and green buttons like Christmas decorations was getting short, and the brown one with the beige silk collar made her feel as drab as a cloudy day. Missus Frances passed her a long, green dress, a dark blue coat and a brown hat.

Clarissa spied a pair of black-tapped, pink satin shoes lying carelessly on the floor. She couldn't take her eyes off them. They were high around like open-necked boats, and had long toes topped by tiny, pink sequins shaped into flowers; in the middle of each flower was a bead. They were the most beautiful shoes she had ever seen.

"Missus Frances," she called, her longing for them so great that she could barely swallow, "may I have those pink Sunday shoes?"

The mistress shook her head. "Even if you could fit your feet into them, you can't walk in them."

"Please, Ma'am, may I have them just to sit in?"

"And let someone else's feet go bare because of vanity?"

"If they don't fit anyone, may I have them?"

The mistress shook her head, her grey eyes weary-looking. "I'm sorry, Child."

Clarissa left the room and made her way to her dormitory wishing she could stamp her feet into the shape of everyone else's. But there were other things to think about. There were only a few days left until the boat came for her. She would have to say goodbye to the girls in her dormitory. Not that they cared. She didn't know how she was going to tell Cora.

"I'm going home," she told the girls that night, her chin up. They looked at her from their beds. They were silent at first. Then Becky, who rarely spoke to her, rushed to wrap her arms around her. "You don't need to go home. Sure, you've got a fine fit here."

All the girls' faces softened towards her. She knew then, the longing they had without the hope she had. Their mothers were dead. They had snitched on her and accused her of being a pet, but now that she was leaving, going to a real home, they came to hug her, one by one. "I wish I had a real mother," Imogene said wistfully.

"Yes, Emma Jane," Becky said. She pulled on an eyelid as if she had something in her eye.

"Let's play jackstones, Clarissa, before you go," Imogene suggested, beckoning all the girls in the room to join in. *Imogene isn't so bad when she smiles,* Clarissa thought. Imogene's fingers were long and knobby-knuckled, and the marbles stayed on the back of her hands. It was easy for her to win the game – and Clarissa's cat's-eye. "Take your favourite marble home, Clarissa," Imogene said, letting it slide off the palm of her hand into Clarissa's lap.

Clarissa dropped the marble into her pocket. "Try to walk on my crutches," she said softly. "Have a turn, all of you. Whoever does it best can have my bumblebee marble."

"Your bumblebee marble!" The girls' voices rose together.

They were all red-faced by the time they had stumbled across the room. "I wish I'd known how hard it is getting around that way," Imogene said in a meek voice.

The other girls nodded when Imogene added, "Keep your bumblebee marble, too."

Clarissa tried not to cry, but tears suddenly filled her eyes and ran down her face. Missus Frances, passing the open door, shook her head and said in a sad tone, "If I were leaving, I would cry a barrel of tears."

Clarissa lifted her head. "And make more work for God."

Missus Frances's forehead creased. "Why, Child, whatever do you mean?"

"Nurse Smith told me that God bottles everyone's tears," Clarissa explained. *He must be the only one who cares about the tears of orphans,* she thought. She had cried so many tears that all the water draining out should have shrunk her. Instead, crying made her body feel heavier and heavier.

The mistress came into the room and put her hand on Clarissa's shoulder. Impulsively, she said, "You left the safety of your mother's body to be born, and the safety of your house to get help for your paralysis, but you did not leave your mother's heart. You will find yourself in it when you go home."

Clarissa looked up, her heart swelling with hope.

29

MYSTERY BOX ON
TEA HOUSE HILL

The next morning, Clarissa went outside to sit on the orphanage steps. *I should tell Cora I'm going home,* she thought reluctantly, *I'll have to tell her.* She watched Ben and Johnny clumming around, locking arms with each other on the ground until Jakot came running with a mouse by the tail. The boys scattered, squealing. Jakot kept running until he got to the landwash, where he tossed the mouse into the water. Even though the boys were working in the mission barn, milking cows and doing other jobs the caretaker had for them, they still found time for mischief.

The sweet smell of the newly scythed grass the boys were raking and tossing hit Clarissa's nose. She heard Uncle Aubrey calling sternly, "Boys! Be quick with the grass. 'Tis on for burning up in the sun, and when you put the hay in pooks, don't round it too much before it's high or you'll have the boar's back." Clarissa knew that "the boar's back" meant a job done poorly.

Just then a cloud came, wrapping the sun and cooling the air. Clarissa no longer needed to squint against bright sunlight. She looked towards Cora, high in the air on a swing, her lemon-coloured dress like a splash of sunshine. Clarissa drew a deep breath and called: "I'm going home – to my real home."

The swing settled into a straight pull. Cora jumped off and ran towards Clarissa, her long, dark legs rushing like whips through the air. "You're goin' home where yer mother and father are. I knew you would someday," she added in a resigned voice. She flounced down on the grass, gasping for a good breath. "You can go home, but I can't; I can never go home. After Pappa died and Momma moved us here, someone else took to living in our house." She smiled lamely. "We can always be sisters of the heart. That sounds poetic."

"It is," Clarissa said, relieved at Cora's response. A thought jarred her. *What if the mistresses send me away before Cora and I get to go back up on Tea House Hill?*

Clarissa looked at Cora. "We have something to do before I go home. We have to sneak up to Tea House Hill."

"Maybe today. It's Wednesday – Woden's Day," Cora suggested impulsively.

"Woden's Day?" Clarissa wrinkled her nose.

"Odin's Day, then. The day the moon was created. 'Twas in a library book I just read – about Odin, a Norseman god."

"Reverend Penny would call Odin godless, so don't breathe that name into his ear," Clarissa warned her. "Some things are best kept to ourselves."

Cora's eyes flashed. "Sure, you won't catch me breathing that into Reverend Penny's ear."

Clarissa suddenly thought of Treffie. She had not told anyone – not even Cora – that she had heard Treffie call her

name as plain as day the afternoon she died. She hoped
Treffie was looking down on her from somewhere beyond
the sunsets and sunrises. She knew that when someone you
love dies, you have to carry the weight of their life inside your
heart. *It's not so heavy if you let them dance there,* Clarissa
thought. She often imagined Treffie as one of the Merry
Dancers.

Cora's voice cut into her musings. "The mistresses won't
get ampery with *you*, but they'll punish me if we're caught
goin' up on the hill. Now that yer goin' home, they'll treat you
easier."

Clarissa grimaced. "I wouldn't count on that." Then she
smiled broadly. "We want to go up to see if the box is still
there, so what are we waiting for?"

Taking a deep breath, Cora said, "I've been not wanting
to go up for fear 'tis a fairy box, but now that yer leaving I'm
hauling up my courage. But," she added, "I'm turning my
sweater inside out for good luck." She pulled her sweater over
her head as she walked backwards.

"You and your fairies." Clarissa shook her head and started towards the gates. Cora followed, pulling her sweater back
on, inside out. She ducked to avoid a stick young Johnny was
throwing into the air and catching.

"It could be Pandora's box!" Cora said under her breath.
They had both read about Pandora.

"It's not." Clarissa's eyes narrowed. "Hers was already
opened, and all the evil in the world let out. That's why we
have boys like Jake, The Great Big Snake."

Cora added, "It can't be St. Patrick's box, the one the
Irish saint threw into the sea after slammin' the lid on the
snakes. There's no shamrocks on it."

The girls chattered about the box until they started up

Fox Farm Hill. They stopped to sniff the white flowers of Indian tea casting its dainty fragrance.

Cora, looking pale, went a ways, then stopped to lean against a big spruce tree, her breathing noisy. "By the time I finish climbing Tea House Hill, I'll be looking for me breath."

"I want you to be better of your influenza or bronchitis, or whatever it is you got," Clarissa said impulsively.

"I will," Cora promised, "when this bad spell goes away." She pulled out a hair from the top of her head and pushed it up under the loose bark of the tree. "Here," she said, putting her hand over Clarissa's, "say with me 'In the name of the Father, Son and Holy Ghost – be gone.'"

"You are my best friend, Cora Payne, but I'm not sure we should be mixing magic cures with Christian prayers. Ask your mother to stir molasses and turpentine bladders in hot water. That might loosen your breath."

"Come on," Cora implored. "Let's forget about everything but the box."

The girls went on their way in silence, hoping no one had been up to the Tea House since their last visit.

When they reached the Tea House, their mouths dropped open at the sight of the place: it looked worse than it had the last time they were there. Now it was like a trapper's squat. A windowpane was broken and leaves rustled against split steps leading to the broken door. Shards of dishes lay in the fading grass as if a prowler had taken them from the Tea House and strewn them around. The curtains had been torn down from the window and the chairs overturned, but the floorboards were still in place. The girls' eyes bored into each other's for only a moment. Then Cora set a chair back up on its legs for Clarissa to sit on. She got down on her knees to lift up the boards. She hesitated, then blurted, "For all we know, the devil, himself, could be in there with his hooves and his horns and a big prong."

Clarissa reasoned, "What would the devil be doing shut up in a box? He's out in the world stirring up mischief in the minds of people like Jake and Imogene. Likely all we've got is an old tea chest; there's probably nothing in it but bugs. You don't have to open it if you're too scared."

"But I want to open it." Cora turned her head and looked up at Clarissa, her eyes as clear as saltwater crystal. "I've made up my mind."

Clarissa leaned forward and lifted her crutch. She tapped the box. "There's no one home," she joked.

"I'll get a sharp piece of rock," Cora said. She hurried out of the Tea House, taking her time going down the ramshackle steps. Clarissa sat as still as the box until Cora came back, out of breath and holding a rock. She scrooched down on her knees and bent towards the lock, banging on it.

"Don't wake the dead," Clarissa said, laughing. She leaned back, recoiling against the back of the chair as one rusty hinge flew off with a ping. Tiny screws scattered along the floor. Cora banged on the other hinge. It popped up, its screws dropping away. Cora's eyes looked as big as pools with blue flowers floating in their centres as she bent back on her heels. "If I lift the cover, we could be looking at filthy clobber cast off from some rat-infested ship."

The girls faced each other, locking eyes. Clarissa leaned forward, holding her breath. She stuck her crutch under the lid and it flew up. With one voice, they exclaimed, "Seaweed!"

"Seaweed as brittle as old leaves," Cora said flatly.

"Seaweed can cover things," said Clarissa. She grimaced

at the sight of dead insects flattened inside the lid like pressed grey flowers. Cautiously she reached in and lifted out the dry, rusty-coloured seaweed. She fell back squealing as a large, round-bodied, black spider ran across her hand. Icy fear slithered down her spine.

The girls sat back shuddering, both afraid to reach their hands and grab the seaweed. Cora took a twig and pushed it timidly into the brittle covering, lifting it.

"An old sealskin coat and a beaver hat. And a hide of some kind," Clarissa said. "We haven't waited all this time not to see the bottom of the box."

Cora went outside. Soon she was back with a large stick. She shifted it under the hat and tossed it on the floor. Then she pushed her stick under the mildewed and fousty-smelling coat and hoisted it out. She gasped as a gold coin flew into Clarissa's lap.

Cora dropped the coat and grabbed the coin. Her hand closed over it. Without looking down, she muttered, "It's the devil, himself, on it, I'm sure."

"Look at it," Clarissa said impatiently. "Find out if it's the devil or a king."

Cora opened her hand and squinted. She rubbed her sleeve over the rough and dirty coin in her palm. There's 6p and an angel and a dragon on one side, and a man on the other. It's probably too old to be worth anything. Still," she brightened, "I could keep it – sort of as a good luck charm like a rabbit's paw."

"The rabbit wasn't too lucky or it wouldn't have lost its paw," Clarissa retorted. "Look what happened to Ben. Maybe his mother carried a rabbit's paw, and that's why he was born with a harelip." She turned to look at the coat. "There may be other things in the pockets."

"I can't put my hand in there," Cora squealed. "There's sure to be a mouse or some other frightful creature hiding – or dead."

The girls faced each other; each wanted the other to go first.

"I'll do it." Clarissa's face had a determined look. *I might find enough gold coins to be able to hire a great surgeon to make me well,* she thought. She slid off the chair to the floor and slipped her hand into the opening, closing her eyes as squeamishness filled her. Her hand went deep, filling the pocket. One finger went though a hole. She pulled back her hand, disappointed.

"Empty," she said glumly.

"Sure, there's another pocket. Since you ventured yer hand inside one, you may as well do the other one," Cora said hopefully.

Clarissa slowly slipped her hand into the other pocket, praying that a mouse or some other furry creature wouldn't squirm under her fingers. Her fingertips touched something smooth and hard between the cold, damp linings. Her hand closed over it and she pulled it out.

"Look! I put my hand into that old trapper's coat for a piece of rock!" She threw it on the floor in disgust.

Cora picked it up. "Not just a piece of rock," she said in awe. "'Tis the same kind of flint as Peter carried."

"It can't be," Clarissa said in scorn. She stopped then, remembering her dream.

"Sure, there's a hole in it," Cora added, reaching around her neck and taking off a string of rawhide. A piece of flint hung from it. She laid the two pieces together.

"Exactly!" Cora screamed. She lowered her voice and said sadly, "Maybe Peter was right. He believed his people came from far away beyond the water's reach. We should have gone up and opened the box before. We could have given Peter the missing piece of flint; then he would have had better luck."

Realizing that something didn't add up, Clarissa was blunt: "Where did *you* get the flint?"

Cora hung her head and sighed. "You know I was on the beach the day Peter died." She took a deep breath and confessed in a guilty voice, "The boys were building a bough wiffen tilt. They had just come with a wheelbarrow of posts. I heard the dogs howling, and I dared Peter to hang from the kennel upside down." Her voice fell until Clarissa could barely hear it. "The dogs grabbed him. I heard him scream. I wanted to run – to tell someone, but I couldn't move at first; my legs were locked up. The next day after the dogs had been shot, I went down to the beach. That's when I saw the flint on the rawhide string. It must have come off over Peter's head when he was hanging upside down. I put it around my neck so I could pray for forgiveness."

Clarissa's eyes brightened in hope. "That's why you've been so sad and tired. It's not just your cough. But everyone has a choice on a dare. Peter made his."

Cora seemed relieved. She smiled, and Clarissa was glad they had opened the box. She leaned over to look down into it. There was something white and round, like the base of a jug, among the seaweed left at the bottom.

"I'll get it," Cora said, laying the two strings of flint on the ground. She reached to lift up the object, grunting as her hands went around it, her fingers slipping into openings. "I should have pulled up extra floorboards. 'Tis hard to reach, but I think it's a jug with holes in it." She lifted the thing into the light.

As Cora pulled herself up on her knees with the object in her hands, Clarissa shrieked. Cora looked in horror at what she was holding. Her hands went weak and the object rolled from them and down on the trapper's coat and into the beaver hat.

"It looks like someone's head," Clarissa said faintly, "without any skin."

"Without any eyes," Cora added with a shudder.

"Without a tongue to tell us who owned it," Clarissa ended bleakly.

They sat looking into each other's face, until Cora whispered, in a quavering voice, "It's likely Peter's father's head in that box – got himself murdered by Indians or white trappers for stealing their furs and such. If 'tis so, then Peter's and his father's flints can settle into one piece in the box."

"Why are you whispering?" Clarissa asked.

Cora stared through the door into the woods that surrounded the Tea House. Without turning her head, she said, "I forgot to bring some bread."

"I'm not hungry," Clarissa answered impatiently.

"For the fairies. Sure, I hear them blabbering in the trees. Listen!" Cora's eyes stood still in her head. "You can't see them, but they're dancin' in the woods."

"Your ears must be keener than my eyes then. A bear is likely talking to itself about having us for supper." Clarissa rolled her eyes.

"Maybe someone followed us. Jakot! Or Peter's ghost!" Cora whimpered.

"Then let's get out of here," Clarissa said. "Drop everything back down in the box."

"Even the coin?" Cora asked in a quivering voice.

"Even the coin." Clarissa's words pressed down on Cora's.

Clarissa flinched as Cora slipped a stick into an eye socket and lifted the skull. She expected it to break apart like pieces of chainies, but it didn't, and Cora dropped it back down into the box. The coat and beaver hat followed. Then she tossed in the coin and the pieces of flint. "This is where everything belongs," she said, firmly pressing down the lid. "Too bad we don't have some large nails to clint it." She covered the box with branches, and fitted the floorboards back in place.

They started down Tea House Hill, passing the Grenfell castle without looking towards it, without speaking, as if some mystery had invaded their beings. Flowers, dancing in the breeze, made everything seem peaceful. But inside, Clarissa felt as if the daylights had been knocked out of her.

As they neared the orphanage, Cora said, "'Tis best for us not to tell anyone about this."

"Let's not," Clarissa agreed.

"I'd like to know where that box came from, all the same."

Clarissa shook her head. "We can imagine what we like, but we can't know everything. Life isn't like books with an end to mysteries. It's best that way. We can spend our lives thinking back and wondering . . . making our own endings, and changing them any way we want."

"It's good to no longer have to wonder what's in the box," Cora said in relief. "We don't have to find the nerve to open it and it's nice to have a secret that is still a mystery."

Clarissa agreed. "One that will lead our minds off in all directions when we have nothing else to do but think."

As they went towards the orphanage, Clarissa's eyes got a faraway look. *Soon,* she thought, *I'll open a box of words in a house full of people. I'll enter my family's lives and my family will tell me why I have been here all this time.*

30

ON HER WAY

The next day dawned at the dormitory window like a silver light shining from Heaven. Clarissa's roommates surprised her this time by waiting until she was ready. Then they all made their way downstairs together.

Clarissa was finishing her breakfast when she felt tears surface. She squeezed her eyes tight; when she opened them, they were wet. As soon as the children were dismissed, she went outside and leaned on the veranda rails. A heavy feeling settled around her heart and rose in her throat, thick as the fog that was beginning to batten the harbour.

She turned around and went inside to her locker. She lifted the lid and looked at her treasures: books, a toy watch from her mother, her beaded necklace, the doll and cradle Miss Brown had given her, a piece of sparkling blue-green stone she had picked up near the beach. Fire rock, the Indians called it.

There were reminders of the caretakers. Clarissa still had the lucky rock Uncle Aubrey gave her. His voice was stronger than a whip, and worked as well as a lashing. Mr. Manuel, the caretaker before Uncle Aubrey, though kind to Clarissa, and the other girls, had often had a crack at the boys. More than once he had made their smiles disappear and their tight lips erupt in a cry. Clarissa had heard him defend himself to Dr. Grenfell. "With so many children to keep reined, we have to be tough."

The doctor, having a mind for listening to orphans and discerning the truth, dismissed him. His departure had brought a look of relief to the boys' faces and a frown to the mistresses' and housemothers' faces, as if their tasks at hand had widened.

Mr. Manuel had once given her a two-cent copper. "A big, brown cartwheel penny for your thoughts," he had said with a chuckle, "though I don't think yours can be bought."

A penny for some buttons, she had thought. She bought a shiny black French jet button and a calico button at the Grenfell shop. She had given the calico button to Treffie to put on her bracelet of buttons. A few days after Treffie died, Clarissa had noticed that the nail fastening the front of Hipper's overalls was gone; in its place was a large button that looked like the one that had been on Treffie's father's over-coat. It wouldn't be there long. The housemother had sewn a button on Hipper's overalls before; he had twisted it off and gone back to his nail fastener.

"May I have one of Treffie's buttons?" Clarissa asked Miss Elizabeth one day when she was thinking hard on Treffie.

"The buttons have all been put to good use, the same as Peter's belongings," she was told. "Young Johnny, who is big for his age, is wearing poor Peter's shoes and clothes."

Clarissa was holding the beads with the cross on them when she heard Cora's voice behind her. 'I won't ever see yer again. I won't, will I?"

Clarissa turned slowly towards Cora, who was leaning against the door frame with a sad, questioning look. She faced her, not sure what to say. She could not make promises she might not be able to keep.

"Missus Frances made Suzy and me go to the hospital for tests this morning. I heard the nurses at the hospital talking about tests Suzy had before. They think her lungs are clotted – she'll likely die in a year. I'll likely die too," Cora added in a resigned voice.

"In a year!" Clarissa reached instinctively to put her arms around her friend. She fell flat on the floor. "You can't ever die!" she cried. "We are sisters in spirit – sisters of the heart."

Cora reached down to help Clarissa up on her crutches. She drew back as coughing racked her body. Coughs and sobs mingled.

Cora stopped coughing and said in an even tone, "God will take me to Heaven where my father is. I'll just go a little earlier than you."

"But you have to live here first. There's lots of time to go there. You should be at least as old as Mrs. Grenfell and have as many children."

Clarissa could understand why Cora's mother sometimes seemed sad. She was likely thinking of her husband gone, thinking of Cora, and little Suzy going. . . . Sometimes Mrs. Payne looked to be fading.

Cora began coughing again and didn't stop until blood foamed on her lips. She dug into her pocket for her brown handkerchief and wiped her mouth. She sighed. "I tried to not to cough in front of the mistresses, but they found out that I've been having coughing spells."

"You may need to have your turn at the hospital, Cora," Clarissa said honestly.

"Don't be telling me that. I don't want to go there and then disappear like Treffie."

"Treffie was run down when she came. Then she got TB meningitis. That killed her quick. I heard Ilish and Georgia talking."

Sadness closed around the two girls; Cora's eyes bubbled with tears. "I want you to stay here."

"But I can't, not for long."

"How long is long?" Cora's voice sounded muffled.

"I don't know. Whenever I'm called to go on the boat. Maybe tomorrow."

Clarissa had often stood on the wharf feeling dizzy as she looked up at the spar of the *Prospero,* and its flag, the Union Jack, waving in the wind. Now she was going away on the *Meigle,* a big ship that voyaged among icebergs.

The next morning, Cora emptied Clarissa's locker and brought its contents to the dormitory. Georgia was helping Clarissa get ready for home. She was combing Clarissa's hair and prating on about how the mistresses let her grow her hair long enough to swing like a rope now that she was old enough to take good care of it. She was telling Clarissa that Dr. Grenfell was sending her to study nursing in the United States when Miss Elizabeth rushed into the room. "The *Meigle* has come before it was expected. You must hurry."

"But my corsets! I need to buckle them on!" Clarissa sputtered.

"You don't have time," the mistress said sharply, grabbing

the surgical corsets and shoving them into Clarissa's arms. "Here, carry them. Georgia will take your bag."

There was no point in arguing. Clarissa tucked the corsets under her arm, feeling as humiliated as if they were her navy drawers. She squeezed her arm against her body, hoping she wouldn't drop the undergarment.

She sweated her way along the gravel road in her heavy coat. She stopped to look back over her shoulder at Cora standing by the orphanage gates, sad and silent.

* * *

The sun was sitting in a blanket of fog as if it had just awakened and was getting ready to roll out of bed as Clarissa was lifted into a lifeboat, which was winched up to the *Meigle*, a long and ugly steamer. Able-bodied passengers walked up the rope ladder. A gust of wind swung the ropes and Clarissa heard squeals from passengers. A sailor shouted, "Davy Jones, here I come – down into your locker room!"

The *Meigle*, a Union Jack flying from its spar, bid farewell with three blasts of a horn. It was an eight-hour trip to Battle Harbour, where Clarissa would disembark and wait for another boat to take her the rest of the way home. She was glad when the sun broke through the fog, sending clouds drifting across the sky like fluffy little creatures on their own journey somewhere. She wouldn't have wanted rain from a dark, cold sky to mingle with her flowing tears as the schooner voyaged past the orphanage. The orphans had gathered on the banks to wave goodbye. Instead of the brown handkerchiefs they always carried, they lifted white handkerchiefs in the air as if they were sails helping Clarissa on her way. All except Cora, who waved a brown handkerchief.

Standing on the deck high above the waves, Clarissa looked towards the children, letting her tears fall freely. She knew they would miss her. She would miss them terribly, even the ones who had made fun of her and called her a cripple. But she would miss Cora most of all.

As the ship moved out to sea, she stood at the rail, one hand on a crutch, the other holding tightly to a belaying pin. Gulls kliooed above waves swimming in the bay like fish, white finned against dark water.

"Ha, 'twon't be the best night to see the *Titanic*," predicted a rough-looking sailor who came to stand beside her. He pulled on his overgrown beard. "'Tis a good omen if we do. But it bes always on a calm night, like the April one when she sank. Its ghost bes so big it could knock a ship flat in the water. But it just passes on by."

The sailor helped Clarissa down dirty stairs to a small seat where someone had laid her bag. She sat down and placed her crutches beside her. Then she pushed her corsets into the bag. She leaned back with the bag in her arms, holding everything that was familiar.

"Lie here," the sailor said, putting a pillow on the seat. She lay down, exhausted with thoughts of going home. Her mind felt as if it were latched to St. Anthony like an ose egg to a rock as the ship moved out to sea, bumping over waves, slapping down on them as if they were giant boulders. She shuddered to think that she was in the middle of a large ocean in a ship that could sink like the *Titanic*, whose grave she hoped she wouldn't have to cross. She curled up on the seat, her braces still on her legs, and let her body go limp. "*Hush, hush, sharp wind knitting seas*

*into a hundred knots. Drift, drift, sweet wind; flow free
your scarf of a hundred breaths,"* she murmured as she
drifted into sleep.

Clarissa knew nothing else until a voice hauled her to her
senses.

"You'm a sleepyhead fer sure," the sailor was saying.
"But yer here now in Battle Harbour ter wait for der *Segona*
to take yar home. So, 'op, 'op."

She followed him upstairs and was winched down into a
smaller boat that would take her ashore. In the twilight, she
stared at Battle Harbour, a cold, empty-looking place. There
was hardly a tree in sight. Outside the hospital there were only
a few crude dwellings, including fishing stages; the stink of fish
was overpowering. The sailor helped Clarissa onto
Croucher's wharf. She steadied herself and followed him over
a bumpy path to the nursing station.

Nurse Barter, one of Dr. Grenfell's summer nurses,
greeted her with a smile and a nod. "Come with me; your
room is all ready upstairs."

The nurse stopped outside a small room. Inside, a young
girl was already asleep in a narrow bed. A lit lamp stood on a
tall bureau.

"Goodnight then," the nurse said, and left. Clarissa
stared at the girl. There were sores on her hands and her
mouth. Clarissa went into the room shuddering at the
thought of catching the girl's sores. She was tempted to
sleep on the floor. Instead, she slid into bed with her head
at the foot and curled herself up like the tail of a cooked
lobster. Despite her nap on the schooner, she soon fell
asleep.

"Come on then, down to the kitchen for breakfast,"
Nurse Barter called, stirring Clarissa from sleep. The other

girl was already gone from the bed, evidence of her illness left behind on the pillow.

Clarissa washed her face in the basin sitting on a nightstand beside the bed, wiping away the salty crusts of dried tears around her eyes.

She was coming down the stairs when she saw Dr. Grenfell at the bottom, speaking to a German doctor she'd seen once before at the orphanage. Dr. Grenfell looked up, and Clarissa's smile vanished when he remarked to the other physician, "She was a mess when we got her."

What does he mean by that remark? she thought, as she made her way to the kitchen. She sat at a small table and Nurse Barter brought her bread and jam from the pantry.

* * *

Dr. Grenfell asked Nurse Barter to get Clarissa ready for an examination in the infirmary. The German doctor was in the room with them when Dr. Grenfell said again, "Yes, she was a mess when we got her." The nurse helped her climb up on the table. Dr. Grenfell looked at her body and wondered aloud about the dents in her hip. "Why do you have hollows in your hip? Were they made by running sores? Oh, I know," he murmured sheepishly. "I did that. I put them there myself when I was trying to stretch the muscle."

Clarissa remained calm during the doctors' examination, displaying the sunny disposition she was supposed to have, but that night she lay on the bed crying as Dr. Grenfell's words banged at her mind. After awhile, her eyelids slipped together like curtains against the light, and she fell asleep.

***

Night after night, she hobbled back and forth across the
veranda at the nursing station, crying. Her heart longed for
St. Anthony. One evening she watched the green and laven-
der Northern Lights: Merry Dancers prancing across the
sky, promising that the next day would be calm and sunny.
Another night, the moon was so full and seemed so near,
she reached up her hand as if she could hold it like a sand
dollar.

On the tenth day, Clarissa saw the *Segona* cutting through
the waters, its flag flying and spars lit up with multicoloured
lights. Her heart felt as if it were caught in her throat. She was
really going home. Her insides seemed to fill with fluttering
moths, their discarded caterpillar bodies heavy in the pit of her
stomach.

"Come on," Nurse Barter urged Clarissa. "Make haste!"
She grabbed Clarissa's arm, pulling on her, hardly giving her
time to get the crutches under her arms. Once she got to the
wharf, a rough-faced man lifted her into a small boat, and the
crew rowed them out to the *Segona*.

Clarissa had just gotten settled in the bunk of a deck cabin
when she was called for supper. The dining room had two long
tables: one for the passengers, and one for the captain and the
crew. The steward, dressed in a spotless white coat, asked her
if she wanted fish or roast beef. The main course came with a
salad topped by the cook's special dressing. There were soda
biscuits and cake or pie for dessert. For a moment she forgot
about everything but the food. She ate her supper joyfully, finishing it off with what the cook called a "civil" orange. Miss
Elizabeth would have called it a Seville orange.

The next morning when she went for her breakfast, she was happy not to have to eat porridge. She filled up on milk, toast, eggs and bacon as she sat facing the porthole. Suddenly the sight of waves splashing against the porthole made her stomach lift and turn. A voice that sounded as if it was a long ways off called out, "See that container, with the cardboard lining, down be yer feet? Dat's fer yucking in." She retched into the gum bucket, feeling as if her insides would split open with the force.

The steward hurried towards her with a wet cloth. "Yesterday it was so windy there was a lop on me soup, but today, me girl, 'twill be calm enough for you to stare the sea in the face and show it yours mirrored dere as plain as day. We'll 'ave a relish for yer puddick: a fine meal of Jiggs dinner." The thought made Clarissa's stomach roll like the schooner.

From then on, she lay in her bunk without washing or changing her clothes and without eating. When her stomach settled a bit, thoughts of the strangers she would soon meet drifted into her mind. She remembered Missus Frances telling her, "Clarissa, you are going home to be with people to whom you belong."

But I don't know those people, she thought. *I don't know what it feels like to belong to someone.* Her heart leaped. *Maybe I'll have a sister who will share a bed with me. She'll curl around my back and wrap her arms around me when I'm having bad dreams. We'll be spoon sisters.*

One memory swirled inside her head until it became a clear image. She and her parents were in a little dory; they were going to Wild Cove on a picnic. The dory moved through the water, tickling it into laughter. When they reached the beach, Clarissa's mother jumped out into the shallow water and lifted her out of the boat. She waded ashore, holding Clarissa in her arms, while Clarissa's father hauled the dory onto the beach. They settled on a grassy mound and ate a lunch of bread slathered in molasses, and dried caplin her father roasted on a fire. Clarissa sat on a log and watched her parents swim. She touched a weed that had pretty, white flowers, and then put her fingers to her mouth. The yellow dust from the flowers made her stomach sick – the way she was feeling now.

The creak of the cabin door opening startled Clarissa as she lay curled around herself.

"Sure, 'tis a sad little gurl you be," a gruff voice said.

She looked up to see Captain Simmons. His head was topped with a hard cap trimmed with a gold braid matching the ones on the sleeves of his blue uniform. Clarissa thought it dressed up his face in a royal way. "Yes," she answered in a muffled voice. A tear slipped from the corner of one eye and rolled down her cheek into her mouth.

"But yer goin' home."

"I thought I was, but now I know I'm leaving home. I won't know anyone, and no one will want a stranger." She began to sob.

"Yer family is bringing home their own flesh, a part of 'em dat was missing. Just like a part of you have been missing all dese years. I've met yer farder, sure, the train engineer – and a right nice man." His voice softened. "Dry yer eyes, me maid. You'm too pretty a gurl to let yer eyes fill with water. The salt'll fade the blue." He squinted. "If yer eyes was blue, but yers is as brown as earth."

She didn't answer, but she let him wipe her eyes dry with his red handkerchief. When he tipped his hat to her, she smiled and settled down on her bunk and went past the grinding, trembling sounds of the boat into a deep sleep.

She slid into a wild dream. Viking warriors had pulled all the nails out of the schooner. It fell apart, dropping her into the Atlantic Ocean. She drifted on a boat rib. It slipped under the Tea House floor into the mysterious box. Her body was suddenly wrapped in musty fur, her head inside a skull.

31

A SISTER'S CONFESSION

Clarissa's eyelids flew open as her body made an abrupt shift in the bunk with the lurching of the schooner. There was a sudden stillness: the engine had been cut. Then came the racket of voices and feet moving, and the clanging of iron chains thrown out to secure the *Segona* to the gump posts of the wharf.

I must be home! I'll see my family soon. A tremor went through her body. *What if I don't like anyone? Worse, what if no one likes me? Will they expect me to walk and run like them?*

She had often imagined running towards her family, her feet light, her arms swinging carelessly, her body unshackled – running straight into her mother's arms. *If only that could be!* She heard people calling from the boat, and the distant sounds of unfamiliar voices answering from shore. A little later, a cabin boy knocked on the door and opened it. He glanced at Clarissa's wrinkled clothes. "I see yer ready, even if 'tis in a sorry state," he said, smiling and raising his eyebrows.

I have been this ready since I left St. Anthony, she could have told him. She would not let him know she had not had a

good wash since the day she waved goodbye to the children at
the orphanage.

The cabin boy picked up her crutches and passed them to
her. Then he grabbed her bag and helped her out of the cabin,
across the deck and down the gangplank. She was helped
ashore by a jolly-looking man in a Lammy coat. The smell of
lamb's wool and sweat filled her nose.

A man and a woman were looking in her direction. A
dark-haired boy hurried to her side. "I'm your brother, John,"
he said, grinning expectantly. Clarissa smiled at him, but she
didn't say a word. It was as if her throat had grown together
over all the words she had wanted to say for so long. John
stooped and picked up the bag lying beside her feet on the
wharf. When he slung it over his shoulder, a cry came from its
depths.

"She's brought home a cat!" John exclaimed, his eyes
wide.

Behind him, her parents smiled. Clarissa stared at them.
She wished she could have cried Momma, like her doll had
inside her bag, – cried Momma and gone straight into her
mother's arms. But then her mother's voice floated on the air
like music: "Welcome home." Her father echoed his wife's
words with a glad look.

"I – I thought – you would be old – older," Clarissa stam-
mered. She had pictured her parents as having wrinkles and
grey hair. Instead, her father's face was smooth and fair, his
hair blond below a cap that looked like a large ose egg perched
on the crown of his head. Her mother was dark-haired and
beautiful. Clarissa hoped that when she grew up she would be
an exact copy of the woman standing in front of her.

As Clarissa and her family made their way along dusty
Station Road, squawking crows lollied across the sky. John

went ahead with Clarissa's bag while her parents stopped to wait as Clarissa crossed the train track. She did this carefully, making sure her crutches didn't catch in the track ties. "Take your time," her father said gently. Her mother looked at her with an encouraging nod. They both stayed in line with Clarissa as she hopped up the road. They followed John, turning down a gravelled path to a white, two-storey house surrounded by trees. Clarissa's heart felt as if it was going to lift out of her into the clouds, and leave the rest of her in a swoon on the ground. She leaned on her crutches and breathed in the sweet scent of roses and honeysuckle.

"I'm Charlie," a young boy called as he hurried around the corner of the house, his face stretched in a grin. When he saw Clarissa's crutches, he shooed away sheep that were running up from the meadow. He stayed close to his sister until she reached the veranda.

John shifted Clarissa's bag and eyed her self-consciously. "I'm next to you. I was born the year after you went away."

Clarissa looked at him, but she still couldn't speak. She followed her mother and father towards the open door of the porch.

Her ears perked at the sound of a train chugging around a curve in the track, its whistle blowing. It brought the familiar feeling of a memory Clarissa had tried to pin down many times.

She stood in the doorway of the house, marvelling that she had finally come home. She suddenly felt that she didn't belong. The people smiling at her were strangers. *I left a place where I didn't belong and now I'm in an even stranger place,* she thought in despair.

She swung her body inside the house and stumbled over to a settee, missing it and landing on the floor. She dropped her head to hide the burst of tears. Her family stood around her, but no one tried to console her. They didn't know her any more than she knew them. They might even think she was a snob when they heard her speak in a dialect different from theirs.

Her mother walked away, going into the kitchen as if she didn't know what to do or say after watching her daughter fall down on the floor she had scooted across when she was a baby. *Nothing has changed – I'm just a big crybaby!* The thought made her cry until her face was drenched. She knew she should wipe the tears away with Nurse Smith's blue handkerchief, but she didn't want to lift her head.

A young woman stood looking at her from the kitchen doorway. She smiled. "I'm Rita, your oldest sister." She nodded towards their mother's back. "Mom's not one for showing her feelings, Clarissa. She never said much after you went away, but you could tell it was hard on her. Now Dad – he's softhearted – used to lie on the couch in the hall with tears streaming down his face. He couldn't stand the thought of you so far away."

Rita pointed to the rest of the children in the room and told Clarissa their names. Gerald was the light-haired baby sitting in a highchair; the toddler was Molly. The girl sweeping mats, who looked a little younger than Rita, was Elizabeth.

Clarissa's brown eyes, as round as the bumblebee marble in her pocket, stared at a girl walking towards her. "I'm Lily," said the girl, with a wide, warm smile. She held out her hand to help Clarissa up. "Come here, you scraggly, little cripple. I'm taking you to the backroom for a good wash. Sure, you've frightened Marie. She's only nine and when she saw you coming over the hill she ran the other way."

Clarissa said nothing as Lily helped her up. She hobbled

after her sister, relieved to be moving away from so many curious eyes.

"We have no flush toilets here," Lily said. "Just a two-hole outhouse in case two people get the runs at the same time." She laughed at Clarissa's look of dismay. "There'll be a chamber pot under your bed, and a kerosene lamp on the bed table so you won't want for light."

"I'll heat some water and fill the tub and you'll get a good scrub," Elizabeth said, coming into the room and pushing her sleeves up to her elbows. "You're a dirty little streel after being on the sea for so long. But you'll soon be as clean as rain."

Clarissa caught sight of herself in the mirror on the wall. She told herself: *Smile at the girl in the mirror and she'll smile back at you. Look at her and see a pretty girl and you will look pretty.*

"Before you start preening in the mirror," Lily said boldly, "let's get rid of this ugly dish."

A bowl of curls fell to the nape of Clarissa's neck as Lily grabbed her brown brimmed hat and exclaimed, "There! That's better."

After Clarissa's bath, Lily brought her brand new clothes. Elizabeth grabbed up the old ones to put with the rubbish in a barrel outside the house.

"Just a minute." Clarissa reached into a pocket of her discarded dress and pulled out the blue handkerchief with its white lace trim. "A keepsake," she explained.

She clutched the handkerchief as she stood in front of the mirror. The heads of the three sisters were framed as if the mirror were a family portrait. *Little Women*, she thought, *that's what we are - like in the book.*

Her sisters and brothers were smiling as she came out of the backroom. As she looked into their faces, she knew that she had never been alone. She could tell by the way they looked at her that their thoughts had travelled the miles from Humbermouth to St. Anthony – that they had *missed* her. She was part of a family, not only in name but in heart.

Rita looked at Clarissa trying to make her way through the living room on her crutches. Her eyes filled with tears. "Oh, Chrissy, little sister, I'm so sorry."

"You do not need to pity me," Clarissa answered primly.

Her sister put one hand to her face. "I don't pity you; you're so pretty. I pity myself. The sight of you will always remind me that I'm to blame."

"To blame? For what?" Clarissa's eyes widened in bewilderment.

"Mommy said you didn't move much after I dropped you. But you're like *that* because of the polio, aren't you?"

Clarissa stared at her. "You dropped me?"

"Yes, when you were a baby." Her words rushed on. "You were so beautiful. I was running up the lane to show you off, to let the other girls see a real doll, one that could cry and open her eyes – not like the dolls they played with. Sally had a baby sister, too, but she had a dumpy face and no hair. I heard Mommy call after me, and when I turned around I tripped against a big rock by the garden gate and fell on top of it with you under me. Oh, I hope I didn't hurt you! I hope that's not why they sent you away. You cried, but you looked the same after I got you back in the house and Mommy laid you in the crib. Then you got a cold; it stayed a long time. Then you couldn't walk by the time you were supposed to. They took you away, and I thought they would fix you. You would walk and run and be like us. Then you'd come home to stay."

Rita stopped and drew in a shuddering breath, blinking hard. "You came home, but you stayed for only a year. That was because Dr. Grenfell asked for you back. I remember Mommy reading the letter and biting her lip, looking up from the page with a troubled face. It seems that the doctor didn't fix you the first or the second time. You're still not fixed." Her hand flew to her mouth as if to drive the last words back inside.

Clarissa stared at her, startled; her eyes filled with anger. She muttered silently: *It is bad enough that I had infantile paralysis, but to be dropped and probably squashed before I had a chance to walk – Maybe Rita's the reason I got paralysis. I want to slap this strange girl!* Her anger was quickly eased by the anguish she saw in her sister's eyes. She found herself smiling at Rita, pitying her for having to carry a load of guilt.

Dr. Grenfell's voice echoed through her mind: *She was a mess when we got her.* He must have thought someone at home had hurt her. Maybe he was trying to protect her. If he had asked, he would have found out it was an accident. And now she was different from her family, more American, more English.

Her thoughts trailed off as she watched her mother set the table. She had always imagined her mother as being like Nurse Smith – the kindest of the kind. She remembered Nurse Smith's words, "My dear child, I visited your house. The place was full of boys and girls. There was likely a half-dozen of one and half a dozen of the other."

Not quite a dozen, Clarissa thought, *and it's a small family compared to a table full of orphanage children.*

A thrill shot through her as her mother beckoned her to take her place. Clarissa hauled herself to the table, letting the crutches lean against the rungs of her chair as she sidled into it. She met her father's eyes shyly. He smiled back, looking satisfied.

She stared at the white bread and fresh cow's meat, food

not plentiful at the orphanage. Then she saw the bowl of sugar in the centre of the table. Everyone looked at her, but no one stopped her as she reached her spoon towards the sweet substance. *This is better than the time I was a sugar cube in a school play,* she thought. The spoon slid deep under the white, grainy crystals. She lifted the spoon towards her and into her mouth. She closed her eyes, not sure if what she would feel first would be the sting of a strap on her hands or the sweet taste of sugar in her mouth. She opened her eyes as the sugar melted on her tongue. No one said anything. She spied a golden glob of butter and pressed her knife into it without hesitating.

"You slice it," her mother told her. "It's cheese."

The thought of breakfast sent an unpleasant churning in Clarissa's stomach. She looked into her mother's warm, smiling face and implored, "I never want to eat porridge again. Please don't make me."

Her mother shook her head and spoke firmly. "Hush, Child, there's plenty of fresh bread and eggs here. You don't have to eat anything you don't want."

Clarissa looked at her, astonished that she would be able to eat what she wanted and leave what she didn't want. She knew then that living at home would be different in many ways from living at the orphanage. "I'll help with the dishes," she offered. "I'll lean on my crutches."

"No, no," her mother said, shooing her away. "You're tired. Go on up to bed."

After she and Rita climbed the stairs to a small bedroom, Clarissa got settled into a warm bed with her sister's help. Rita promised her she would be up later to sleep in the same bed and keep her company. Then she went downstairs.

Clarissa's body tensed under the bedclothes as she waited

for her mother to come – *hoped* she would come. And then she heard the creak of footsteps on the stairs. She let out a contented sigh as her mother came into the room.

"I want you to say your prayers."

Clarissa looked at her and hesitated. Words Protestant orphans had used against her were strung through her mind, flapping like black clothes on a clothesline. She didn't know anything about her mother's faith.

Clarissa waited for her mother to make the sign of the cross as she had done at suppertime. She was ready to copy her. Instead, she smiled and said, "We'll recite "The Lord's Prayer" tonight. You've had a long journey."

Their voices rose together in the familiar words. Clarissa felt all the lonely years rush away as if they had been nothing but an uneasy dream.

"Would you like to know about the orphanage?" she wanted to ask. But she didn't. She imagined what her mother would say: "That's all behind you now: the good and the bad of it."

She reached out her small, brown hand and laid it on her mother's large, white one. Her heart seemed to stand still in her chest as she waited for her mother's hand to turn over and take hers. But it didn't. They were strangers to each other. Her heart sank. She wished sleep would come like a gentle wind, blow her eyelashes shut and whisk her into a place of good dreams.

Then her mother's warm hand turned over and opened. Clarissa's hand slipped into the soft palm; her mother's fingers closed around hers. Brown eyes met blue eyes, and Clarissa felt a surge of joy. All the years that were lost, all the changes in both of them were not things to dwell on. She believed now that time would fly, instead of being dragged through dreary and bright days. And so would her heart even if her body was on crutches. Contentment was a gift she would give to herself in circumstances she could not change.

Under the quilt, her other hand opened and moved away from the blue and white handkerchief. She was no longer Dr. Grenfell's little orphan.

GLOSSARY OF TERMS

Abiver – trembling.

Ampery – inflamed, irritated.

Barrow – a long flannel petticoat.

Barrow – a flat, rectangular frame with two handles at each end.

Bazzing – throwing marbles against a wall (to strike and rebound).

Black Man, The – the Devil.

Blaighard – Unacceptable, shady words. A corruption of black guard.

Bough wiffen – A temporary shelter with no sides, just a roof of boughs over posts. A lean-to.

Buck – steal.

Busy noshers – people who like to feed on gossip.

Cape Anne (Ann) – A fisher's oilskin cap. It had a broad rim that sloped at the back, and ear flaps with strings that tied under the chin.

Chainies – pieces of broken china.

Christmas box – a gift (present) at Christmas.

Chuffie match – a sulphur match used with a tinder box.

Clavie – A custom to open the new year: old blubber casks

were cleaved and set alight, smoking the sky on New Year's Eve.

Clint – to drive nails in wood etc. by bending the heads to keep them in place.

Clumming – wrestling playfully.

Clumpers – loose pieces of ice.

Cobble bread – bread toasted on the buttered side.

Cobby house – a child's playhouse.

Company bread – bread in one's pocket to keep away the fairies.

Conkerbell – an icicle.

Consumption – pulmonary tuberculosis.

Coopy house – hens's shelter.

Copying – jumping from ice pan to ice pan.

Cracknels – rendered pieces of pork fat.

Dodger – a large horn button.

Dunch – used to describe loss of circulation in a body part.

Ferked up – dug up.

Flobbered – slopped.

Footin's – animal tracks in snow.

Gimp – a dress with straps rather than a collar and sleeves, usually worn over a blouse.

Glim – light given off by icebergs in the dark.

Glutches – gulps, swallows.

Gowithy bushes - bog myrtle, sheep laurel, lambkill.

Grippe - influenza.

Grum - sour-faced.

Gump - a wooden mooring post on a wharf.

Guttle - to win an opponent's marbles.

Hagdown - a small seabird. It has a heavy body and its short wings are used as paddles.

Hag-stones - naturally perforated stones, used as charms against witches and for good luck.

Hard tack - a thick, oval-shaped hard biscuit, made without salt or sugar.

Hipper - a bent nail used, in place of a button, as a fastener on clothes.

Hoosing - The use of a short stick in guiding sticklebacks into a bottle or can that has been lowered by a string into a pond.

Hussing - teasing.

In rack - chummy.

Irish Lords - seabirds that live out on the ocean.

Jockabaun - a cruel and mischievous person.

Josh (joist) posts - wooden posts set in holes dug in thick ice, and supported with rocks. The posts were used as markers in a football game. A team player scored by kicking the football between the josh posts of the opposing team.

Klioo - the call of a seagull.

Killick – a homemade wooden anchor with a large, oblong stone in its centre.

Lammy coat – a short, heavy coat.

Lallick – the game of tag.

Lipritty skipping – hopping and skipping about haphazardly.

Lollied – moved slowly up and down like the wings of a bird in flight.

Mainderberries – sweet, minty, white berries growing on glossy leaves overhanging bogs.

Maldow – black, brown and green strands of "beard moss" on tree trunks.

Marming – visiting; going from home to home.

Mazard – head.

Meeami abashish – goodbye for a little while (Canadian Indian).

Merry Dancers – the Northern Lights; the Aurora Borealis.

Mewl – a low cry.

Moidering – muddling, addling.

Mooching – to be absent unlawfully: to go on the pip.

Mot – hole made in the ground to knock marbles into.

Mudsuckers – mythical creatures living in bogs. They will grab anyone who steps in the wet spongy ground.

Ose eggs – sea urchins (corruption of "whore's eggs").

Painter – the rope used to tie a boat to a wharf or stage etc.

Parlour pudge – in the game of hopscotch, either of the two large adjoining squares.

Pips - dots on dice.

Piss-a-beds - dandelion flowers.

Pitty hole - grave.

Poll - top or back of the head.

Pooked - sticking out.

Pooks - hay piled in high heaps.

Pricklies - tiny, yellow-green fish found in ponds.

Puck - hit, strike.

Puddick - stomach.

Puffin - Atlantic sea parrot.

Rafter, to - sheets of ice buckling against other ice, forcing it to rise like a pinnacle.

Ragmoll - dirty or untidy person.

Randying - playing around. Joyriding.

Scrooched - bent down awkwardly.

Sculpins - large, ugly-looking fish with sharp fins.

Sculp pans - pans to hold seal meat after the skin and blubber have been sculped from it.

Smoky Jacks - soft, brown spongy puffballs found in marshes.

Strouters - vertical rails fixed to the side of a fishing stage or wharf.

Summer sickness - diarrhea.

Tatey - potato.

Tolt - a low rounded hill, sometimes with a steep rise.

Trimming – To move along close to, or on the edge of (as in trimming ice pans).

Walloping – moving quickly and clumsily.

Whelping – said of seals, or other animals giving birth.

Sources: *Dictionary of Newfoundland English.* Story, Kirwin, Widdowson. Breakwater, and from the author's manuscript *The Tongue of a Newfoundlander and Labradorian in Word, Phrase, Superstition* ....

ACKNOWLEDGEMENTS

Special thanks to those of Clarissa Dicks's family who wanted Clarissa to be the heroine of and the inspiration for a great story.

I would also like to thank The Newfoundland and Labrador Arts Council for its support.

Finally, thanks go to the staff of Flanker Press, to Dick Buehler, and to Susan Rendell.

Nellie P. Strowbridge, winner of numerous provincial and national awards, has been published nationally and internationally. Her work is capsuled in The National Archives and has been studied in schools and universities as far away as Belarus.

Strowbridge, a former columnist, editorial writer and essayist, has been Writer in the Library, a mentor to young writers and an adjudicator in the Newfoundland and Labrador Arts and Letters Awards. She has also held school workshops and hosted Gabfest for International Women's Day in Cobh, Ireland where she was Writer-in-Residence. The Canadian Embassy in Dublin also sponsored a reading and a reception.

The author is a member of The Writers' Alliance of Newfoundland and Labrador, The Writers' Union of Canada, The League of Canadian Poets, Page One, and The Newspaper Institute of America.

Her previous books include *Widdershins*: Stories of a Fisherman's Daughter, *Doors Held Ajar* (tri-author), *Shadows of the Heart*, and *Dancing on Ochre Sands*.